IN ZACH'S ARMS

ONCE A MARINE, ALWAYS A MARINE

KORI DAVID

In Zach's Arms
By: Kori David

This is an original publication of CoKeA, LLC.

This is a work of fiction. Names, characters, places and incidents either are the product of the author's imagination or are used factiously, and any resemblance to actual persons, living or dead, business establishments, events, or locales is entirely coincidental. CoKeA, LLC or the author, does not have any control over and does not assume any responsibility for third-party websites or their content.

Printed in the United States of America.

www.KoriDavid.com

❀ Created with Vellum

To my husband and tireless supporter – I love you more than I can express in mere words.

To Judy Baker-Manjur, who told me back in college that I should write and then bought a book on how to do it. It's been a long road, but I finally listened.

Also to Marina and Brittany, my extraordinary critique partners – because you both rock my world.

CHAPTER 1

*E*lizabeth Russell was barely through the front door of her small, one-bedroom apartment when she gasped, her feet jerking to an abrupt halt.

"Oh my God," she whispered, her hands covering her mouth.

She scanned the room, taking in the destruction. Sofa and chair overturned; cushions and plants littered the floor. The rich brown soil looked like a bloodstain leaking from the painted terra cotta pot. A faint dust outline clung to the stand where her TV and DVD player used to sit.

Both were smashed.

Elizabeth wrapped her arms around her chest to keep the tremors at bay. A quick glance across the room and a single tear streaked a path down her cheek.

Not the bookshelf. That was the only piece of furniture she'd spent any money on. She treasured her books and loved how the hand-carved shelves seemed to cradle them.

Damn.

Elizabeth threw her purse on the side table by the door and grabbed one of the large brass candlesticks. Hoisting it over her head, she crept further inside. She was scared, but she was also mad. None of this made any sense. She lived in a good part of town, for God's sake. No one else in her building had been broken into. This shouldn't have happened.

Certainly not twice in the same month.

The first time was creepy enough, knowing that some whack-job had pawed through her things—even taking a pair of her favorite silky underwear as some kind of sick little trophy.

A fissure of dread snaked its way down her spine as she wondered what was taken this time. It was nearly impossible not to touch anything. She wanted so badly to pick her stuff up and put it all back the way it used to be, but knew from prior experience that she'd ruin any fingerprints the burglar may have left.

The kitchen sat untouched, but when Elizabeth reached the bedroom, she sank to the floor, her legs no longer supporting her. Shaking her head in denial, acid churned in her stomach.

Her apartment was empty. And devastated.

A tornado going through her apartment couldn't have caused this much damage. The frilly lace curtains were shredded and hung limp on the remains of the twisted, bent curtain rod. Her closet had been ravaged, clothes tossed in every direction. The night stand leaned on three legs against the wall in the corner; the second-hand ceramic lamp she'd been so thrilled to find at the garage sale, lay shattered next to the bed. The seascape pictures from the walls had been ripped down, long jagged slashes through the canvasses.

But the bed...it was almost untouched, except for the rumpled covers and the single yellow rose lying grotesquely mangled on the pillow.

I have to get out of here.

Elizabeth slid up the wall for support and backed out of the bedroom. Tears streamed a hot path down her cheeks as she turned toward the front door and ran.

Grabbing her purse on the way out, she shot down the hallway toward the stairs. Panic clawed its way through her chest as her breath hitched and caught. One flight of stairs down, she tripped on the last step, the momentum throwing her forward. Arms flying out to keep her balance, pain streaked up her leg from twisting her left ankle, but she kept going.

Almost there.

Elizabeth stopped at a light blue door and knocked, while trying to pull in a calming breath. The door at the end of hall sprung wide and Elizabeth stifled a scream. When she saw her neighbor's head appear, she sagged in relief.

"Oh my God, Mr. McCreedy. You scared me."

Mr. McCreedy's suspicious face emerged from his apartment. Narrow eyes and brows tugged inward, he slid his gaze up and down the hall. "And where're you off to? It's a bit late for you, isn't it?"

Mr. McCreedy, a fifty-something man, always had his nose in everyone's business. With his stocky build and light brown hair, he was nice, but he made Elizabeth uncomfortable. Several times, she'd caught him watching her from his window as she unloaded groceries or brought in her dry cleaning.

"Someone broke into my place."

"Again?"

Elizabeth nodded as she kept a death grip on her landlady's doorknob. Knocking harder, her knuckles stung and turned red from pounding. Mr. McCreedy shook his head and mumbled something to himself before shutting his door.

"Keep your pants on, I'm coming," came the terse voice from within.

"Oh, thank you, thank you."

The scrape of metal was followed by a pop and the door swung open. Elizabeth threw herself into the arms of her startled landlady.

⊓⊔

"Ms. Russell?"

Elizabeth looked up into the grim face of the Detective patiently waiting for her attention. She sat in her landlord's apartment, shivering beneath the thick blanket tucked around her shoulders. Cold fear settled in, bone deep, even though it was a balmy seventy-five degrees with the windows open. She didn't even remember her landlady calling the police.

"I'm sorry, Detective, but I don't know anyone well enough to have made enemies." Elizabeth's voice trembled. "I moved to Phoenix little more than a month ago."

"Are you sure there's no one in your past that would wish you harm? A jilted lover or ex-husband?" Detective Wolfe's voice remained calm and soothing, but impatience crept into his tone.

"There are no lovers, jilted or otherwise, Detective. No ex-husbands and no family. I left Casa Grande and a one bedroom apartment six weeks ago. I keep to myself and write."

"What do you write?"

"I'm a freelance writer by trade," Elizabeth shrugged. "I write technical pieces for magazines and I ghost-write for several professionals. It pays the bills."

"I'm sorry to keep hounding you this way, but there must

be something. An average, run-of-the-mill burglar doesn't stab his victim's pictures or mutilate clothing."

He moved to the coffee table and sat in front of her, making eye contact. "They don't take the time to do that. Just in and out with your stuff. This is personal, somehow," he explained. "We found what looks to be semen on the bed. That's a helluva lot more complicated than a smash and grab."

"I think I'm going to be sick," Elizabeth said, closing her eyes and sucking in a deep breath.

"Have you ever had any problems with your clients?"

"No. They all love my work. I'm fast and good at what I do. I've never even had work rejected."

Once the nausea settled, she opened her eyes to stare at Detective Wolfe. He'd arrived after the two patrol officers had thoroughly checked her apartment and taken some initial information.

Elizabeth thought absently that his serious blue eyes were in stark contrast to a mop of unruly brown hair. He was younger than she expected, and handsome, but she felt nothing for him but gratitude that he'd responded so quickly. She racked her brain trying to come up with something to help him, but couldn't imagine anyone trying to hurt her, much less masturbating on her bed.

"I just published my first fiction book. I don't think I told the officers that."

Flipping the page of the notebook he carried, Detective Wolfe scribbled a couple of notes. "What kind of book is it?"

When she didn't answer, he looked up, frowning. Elizabeth could feel the heat move from her toes up to her face, heating the tips of her ears until they tingled. She was proud of her work, but at this moment, given the circumstances, it was embarrassing. "It's um…"

"It might help the case, ma'am," he said when her voice trailed off.

Ducking her head, she whispered quickly, "Paranormal erotic romance."

"Like vampires and werewolves and stuff?"

"More like people with ESP."

"So, mind-reading and telepathy? And raunchy sex scenes?" His eyebrows rose in inquiry. A small quirk of his lips signaled amusement.

"Yes, although my scenes aren't overly racy, considering the genre."

"Hmmm." He wrote a few more notes. "You get any weird correspondence from fans? Hate mail? Threats?"

"It only came out two months ago. I don't have a website yet and my agent is the only one with my address. If he's received anything, he hasn't told me about it." She pushed a hand through her thick hair and shook her head. "None of this makes any sense."

"What about close friends? Anyone else have your address?"

Her mind immediately jumped to Zacharias Steele. Friend wasn't a strong enough word for him. He'd grown up in the crowded foster home next door. They had gone to high school together and had been there for each other though some dark times. Mainly hers. She felt much more than friendship for Zach, but what exactly that emotion was, she wasn't really sure.

Elizabeth shook her head. "I chose a solitary career so that I didn't have to interact with many people. I'm used to being alone, Detective."

Wolfe snapped his notebook closed and nodded. While he didn't look convinced, he finally stopped the interrogation.

"The crime scene techs are going to be in there for several

hours dusting for prints and gathering evidence. Do you have anywhere you can stay for the night?"

Elizabeth's mind immediately went to her friend. Her confidante. The only person who made her feel safe.

Zach.

Once upon a time, she'd offered him her body. He'd offered her marriage instead. She was only eighteen; he was nineteen and going into the Marines and marriage was something that she would never, ever consider. She'd seen what marriage was like for her mother. And she wouldn't ever put herself into that kind of bondage.

So, they'd parted friends. And she'd avoided seeing him in person for a couple of years now. She was a coward and didn't want to risk rejection again. But none of that mattered now.

She needed him.

CHAPTER 2

*T*he driveway of the large cabin had Elizabeth fighting down another bout of nervousness. These nerves had nothing to do with the burglaries and everything to do with the man who lived inside.

She parked her SUV and thanked whatever deity was listening that she owned a four wheel drive. Zach's property sat way off the main road and the driveway had been treacherous.

Elizabeth liked the look of the cabin the minute she saw it. Redwood walls covered the sprawling structure and a wraparound porch dotted with handmade chairs made a cozy impression. A swing swayed lightly in the breeze. It was everything Zach had ever dreamed of and nothing like the foster home he'd grown up in. This place was private, roomy and all his.

She stepped outside and took in a deep breath, feeling her muscles relax. Summer was melting into fall and the air was crisp and pine-scented. Mountains loomed in the distance.

She leaned a hip against the fender, as she debated the best approach. She hadn't told him she was coming. Didn't even know if he had someone in his life who might object to her showing up unannounced, with her suitcase in hand.

It had been forever since they'd talked, even longer since she'd seen him in person. They were different people now.

"This was a stupid idea."

Too bad she had nowhere else to go.

Oh God, this was a huge mistake, Elizabeth thought, rubbing sweaty palms down her jeans. The sun was barely up and she'd been awake all night, first with the police and then debating whether or not to come here.

She reached for the car door, ready to double back to town and check into a motel, when the door to the cabin opened. Zach leaned against the frame dressed in a blue flannel shirt and faded blue jeans. His six-foot-three-inch body filled the doorway as he slowly crossed his arms over his chest. His thick brown hair was shaggy and tousled; it looked as if he'd been running his fingers through it.

Elizabeth straightened and slowly walked toward the porch. This was Zach. The doubt had been a product of an overly-tired imagination. He would help her and make sure no one could hurt her. But first, he was going to growl and grumble and probably yell.

That thought had her smiling.

□□

ZACH HAD WATCHED the slow progress of the SUV from his window as it made its way down the drive. The Sig Sauer 9mm in his hand was a familiar weight and the shotgun behind the door was within easy reach.

Strangers weren't welcome.

When the vehicle stopped and a blonde head emerged, his whole body tensed up and he almost shot himself in the foot. Beth might be average height, but there was nothing average about the curves that graced her body.

The expressions that chased across her face made Zach's eyebrows arch. Dark circles under her eyes showed her exhaustion. Even her posture was sunk in, as if the weight of some burden was on her shoulders.

Something was wrong.

Zach tensed again as he scanned the area, noting the birds still singing. If danger was close, the woods would be quiet. Sensing no immediate threat, he turned back to Beth.

As she reached the porch steps, their eyes met.

"Hello, Zach."

Her soft, sexy voice had a soothing effect on him. It always had. She'd grown up while he'd been gone. The teenager she'd been had given way to a stunning woman.

"Hello, Beth. It's been a long time."

"I hope I'm not interrupting anything." With her hands jammed in the pockets of her jeans, she shot a glance at the partially-opened door.

"And if you are?" he asked, curious to see her reaction.

He wondered if she had the ability to be jealous. Wondered if he even cared about that any longer. He was alone, as usual. But she didn't need to know that.

Yet.

"Then I would, of course, leave. I should have called but I didn't even think..." her voice trailed off.

"You're looking good."

She gifted him with a small smile. "You're not looking so bad yourself, jarhead."

Automatically lifting his hand to his grown out hair, he grinned back. "It's weird having hair again."

The smile slowly faded and she looked over her shoulder

toward the road. She let out a big sigh and turned her liquid brown eyes back to him.

"I'm in trouble, Zach."

Fear. Bright and vivid in her eyes. That's why she was exhausted. And why her whole body was pulled tight.

"Tell me."

"You mind if I sit down?"

He waved her toward one of the chairs on the porch and watched her sit, while he half-sat on the railing.

"My apartment has been broken into twice in the last few weeks." She shuddered. "The police think someone is after me."

"Why didn't you call me?"

"The police are already investigating and I thought this would get cleared up quickly."

Zach shoved his hands in his pockets to hide the fact that they were clenched. If there was one thing in his life that was constant, it was his overwhelming need to protect her. That she didn't call immediately bothered him. Once upon a time he'd been the only rock in her fractured world—a place he wanted to get back to.

She sighed. "I'm here now." Wrapping her arms around her stomach, she shook her head. "I always seem to run to you when I'm in trouble. But, there just isn't anyone else."

Zach pushed away from the rail and moved to her side. Squatting down to her level, he reached out to nudge her chin up so that her eyes met his.

"I will always protect you, Beth. Always."

She pulled her chin away and sat back. "It's pathetic. My parents died and I just expected you to be there for me. Now this, and here I am again, expecting you to take care of it."

"I'm good at taking care of things. It's what I do. And I'm even better at taking care of you." And she knew it, Zach thought, or she wouldn't be here. She tried so hard to be

11

Miss Independent, but when it came down to it, she depended on him, to a certain extent. He would always be there for her.

Because she was his first love.

Moving back to give her some space, he asked, "Tell me about the break in."

ELIZABETH SIPPED the hot coffee he'd poured for her. The wooden chair she'd claimed was comfortable and the fresh air helped her recount the details. They went over it twice. "There's a detective assigned to the case. Detective Wolfe. He's seems young, but competent and extremely thorough. I felt like I was a part of the Inquisition earlier."

"He truly believes this isn't random?"

"Correct. He says it's personal, but I don't know who might want to hurt me. I just don't come into contact with that many people."

"Could be anyone. Some clerk at a store that you frequent. You smile and he thinks it means more than it does. Anyone in your building seem strange?"

Mr. McCreedy gave her the willies, but he'd never said much to her that was weird. Still, something must have shown on her face because Zach's eyes narrowed.

"Who are you thinking of?"

Elizabeth shrugged and sighed. McCreedy rarely spoke, but he watched her.

"It might be important," he prodded.

"It's just this one neighbor...," she shook her head. "It's probably my imagination, but I feel like he watches me. More than the usual nosy neighbor would. His window faces my parking space and, no matter what time I come and go, he's there. Staring."

"What's his name?"

"McCreedy is his last name. I don't know his first name."

"That's a good start. Did you tell Wolfe about him?"

"I didn't even think about it until now. He's lived in the building for years. Bea would have said something if she thought he was a problem."

"Maybe he never had a reason to be a problem until you."

"Nice. So I'm a problem now?"

"Yeah, you are. How many other desirable young women live in that building?"

Trying to ignore the warm tingle his words caused, she said, "It's true, I'm one of the youngest tenants. Bea doesn't usually rent to anyone younger than thirty. She says twenty-somethings are flighty and don't pay the rent on time. But I remind her of her niece in Chicago, so she took a chance on me."

"This guy ever invite you to his place? Or try to touch you?"

"No, and he barely even speaks to me, or anyone else for that matter. I'm sure he's harmless. Probably just lonely."

"Or he's a freak who's planning on taking more from you than just your panties."

"Okay, I was feeling better until you said that."

"I won't sugar-coat this because you're scared. You need to be. Someone out there wants to hurt you and I'm not about to let that happen."

Elizabeth pulled her knees up to her chest. "This is all so ridiculous."

"Give me your keys. I'll move your SUV and get your bags."

"I don't have much with me, just a purse, laptop, and a small bag of clothes."

"Got it," he said, palming the keys. "Go on into the house. The only room made up is the biggest room at the end. Crawl in and get some rest. You look ready to drop."

"'kay."

It wouldn't hurt to close her eyes for a few minutes and catch a nap. Lethargy settled into her body and made her arms and legs feel as if they weighed a thousand pounds. She didn't really sleep these days, but a nap sounded so good.

A nap curled up with Zach sounded even better.

CHAPTER 3

*Z*ach watched Beth sleep on the leather couch. She hadn't even made it to the bedroom. Squatting down to stare into her face, his breath caught. Even as an awkward teen, Beth had been lovely, but she'd grown even more beautiful.

He reached out to brush a strand of hair out of her face. It caressed his rough fingers like silk. It was hard to believe so much time had passed since she was a freshman and he was a trouble-making sophomore from foster care.

The snore made him smile. Beth's full lips were slightly parted. It was good that she was finally getting some rest. The puffiness under her eyes concerned him. Knowing Beth, she probably hadn't slept a full night since the first break-in.

"Time for bed," he said, as he slowly slid his arms under her shoulders and knees.

"Hmmm."

The sexy murmur made him smile, and when he adjusted her in his arms, she cuddled closer. Her breath blew against his neck as he carried her down the hall, causing his body to react. Beth's soft breasts brushed his chest, making it suddenly difficult to walk. It didn't help that he could easily visualize her naked in his arms, their bodies intertwined.

The throbbing in his jeans increased, nudging painfully against the zipper. He'd been a walking hard-on since Beth was in her teens, so this wasn't new for him.

He slid her under the covers, took off her shoes and tucked her in. Then he left the room, grabbed his cell phone and called Mike Hanson. He and "Little" Mike had done two tours in Fallujah together. They'd had each other's backs in some squirrelly situations. Since transitioning into civilian life, Mike had become a cop, moving up to sergeant quickly.

"Hello?" Mike answered, a hint of annoyance creeping through.

"What? I catch you sleeping?" Zach taunted.

"Nah, eating a donut and wasting the taxpayers' money," was the reply.

"You hate donuts and the taxpayers don't pay you enough for the shit you do for them."

"I heard that. What's up, brother?"

"I have a friend with a problem. She's in your jurisdiction and I'm curious about the case and about the lead investigator."

"Give me her name and I'll dig around."

"Thanks, Mike. I'll owe you one."

"Damn straight you will. I'll think of something good to ask for, too."

"You got it."

〇〇

THE SECRET ADMIRER was tired today, but that didn't stop him from wanting to check in on her. That's how he thought of himself. Her secret admirer.

Elizabeth.

Even her name excited him. His visits to her apartment had been spur-of-the-moment, but that didn't diminish the depth of his admiration. He thought she'd liked the rose, even though he'd been hoping to surprise her in person. He'd lost his temper a bit over that. He hadn't meant to do so much damage, but really, it was her fault.

Switching on the monitor, he waited for the tiny camera he'd planted yesterday to power up. He'd placed it in her bedroom in the vent, facing the bed, so that he could watch her any time he wanted. He was happy that the police obviously hadn't found it.

The image finally cleared and showed nothing but rumpled covers and some of the mess he'd made. He felt bad about that. It wasn't like him to lose control like that, but that's what she did to him. It's how she affected him.

She made him crazy.

"Where are you, my Elizabeth?" he whispered.

He assumed she'd be there, cleaning up. Turning off the monitor, he forced himself to relax. She'd be back, sooner or later, and he knew where she'd likely be anyway. That old woman who owned the place was always meddling. She would have demanded that Elizabeth stay with her last night. Maybe Elizabeth was still sleeping.

He would have preferred to watch.

Fingering the silk in his pocket, he pulled out her panties and brought them to his face. He shouldn't have taken them. But even her smell was fresh. Almost virginal. He liked that about her.

It was one of the reasons she was special.

And why she deserved his attention.

◻◻

ELIZABETH WOKE WITH A START, jerking into an upright position. Disoriented, she wondered where she was. Glancing around the masculine room, she sighed in relief. The wood siding, the cedar scent, and the four poster bed...Zach's cabin.

A loud noise blared into the quiet and she jumped.

What was that? The sound happened again and her racing heart began to calm down. It was her cell phone. She fumbled through her purse on the nightstand until she located the ringing phone.

It was already five in the afternoon and the caller I.D. told her it was Jeffrey Jones calling. Her agent. She was supposed to call him yesterday, but between the break-in, the cops, and Zach, it had completely slipped her mind.

"Hello, Jeffrey."

"How's my favorite author?" His nasal voice sounded cheerful.

"Not great. Sorry, I was taking a nap and I overslept; you woke me. I was going to call you later."

Elizabeth valued him as an agent; he was really good. But he tended to be singularly focused. Right now, her career was his focus. He reminded her of a basset hound, with his thinning hair and limpid brown eyes. It wasn't a kind thought, but that's the image that popped into her mind whenever she spoke with him.

"What's wrong? You sound terrible. Is everything okay?" He sounded genuinely concerned.

"My apartment was broken into and destroyed, again." She leaned back against the headboard and shoved a hand through her tangled hair.

"But that's the second time. Have you called the police?"

"Yes. I hope they catch this guy."

"I should hope so. Is there anything I can do to help? Whatever you need, I'm here for you."

"I'm fine and have a place to stay for the moment. So what's up?"

"I e-mailed you the contracts for book three and four and I wanted to make sure you received them and see if you had any questions or concerns. But in light of what's going on, we can hold off on going through them. How about I call your editor to give you some time on the book you're working on now?"

"No, no. I'll get them signed and back to you."

"Great. Do you think you'll be able to meet your deadline?"

"I've got my laptop with me, so I can keep working. I just need this maniac in jail and out of my life."

"This does seem—persistent. If you need anything, please, don't hesitate to call."

She hung up with her agent and turned the phone off. She didn't want to talk to anyone else. Relaxing back onto the soft mattress, she strained to hear some evidence that Zach was close by.

Nothing but silence.

She must have been completely comatose and probably snoring like a drunken sailor when he moved her from the couch to this room. Great impression after not seeing him for years.

But that was the problem.

Her best friend had been in her fantasies for a long time now. He was her dream lover. And that was why she'd been avoiding him for a while now. Not to mention how she'd treated him when he left for the Marines. She cringed at the memory.

She stretched and marveled that she'd managed to sleep for so long. She had slept at least eight hours, straight through. No wonder she felt great, it was the longest stretch of sleep she'd gotten in a week.

She needed a shower and to get out of the clothes she'd been wearing for over twenty-four hours. Once she was clean, she set out to investigate the rest of the house and find its master.

She found two virtually empty rooms and an alcove with double doors. Locked double doors. It looked like the biggest room in the house, next to the living room and kitchen area. How intriguing. Curiosity was her weakness.

Hmmm, wonder what he's got in there?

She'd have to remember to ask Zach about it. The smell of something good cooking coaxed her toward the kitchen as her stomach growled.

"Hey Zach, what do you have hidden behind..."

It wasn't Zach cooking, but a blond giant wielding a very large butcher knife. Letting out a startled yelp, Elizabeth took a step back, her hand flying up to her chest. Blood pounded in her ears and her heart lodged somewhere in the back of her throat.

"Hello, there. Sorry to startle you, but now that you're awake, how do you like your steak? Dead, medium or still mooing?" His soft voice held a hint of Texas twang and the twinkle in his light hazel eyes gave away his amusement over her reaction.

"Um, who are you?"

Still eyeing the butcher knife, she knew Zach would never allow anyone but a friend in the house. God, she hoped she was right, because there was no way she'd get to the door before he overtook her. Screaming was still an option, however.

"He's the ugliest, clumsiest son of a bitch to ever grace the

Corps," Zach said, and Elizabeth released the breath she hadn't realized she'd been holding.

His warm breath tickled her neck a half-second before his arm snaked around her shoulders. As he pulled her back against his broad chest, she instantly relaxed, feeling safe.

"I'll have you know that the ladies like me just fine and, given half a chance, I'll bet I could get this little lady to like me better than you." The giant winked at her. "This idiot doesn't need to come between us -- you come sit with me while I finish cooking up the best steak you've ever tasted."

At six foot five, Zach's friend was wide across the shoulders, narrow in the hips, and covered in muscle. His sandy blond hair looked to be naturally curly and kept ruthlessly short. Good looking and easy with the compliments, he probably had women eating out of his hand. His gray tee was tucked into faded jeans that molded a nice butt and encased long legs ending in scuffed cowboy boots.

"Well, I don't think I can accept a steak from someone I haven't been properly introduced to. I was taught never to talk to strangers." Elizabeth sounded solemn, but only managed it because she was safely anchored by Zach's arm.

"Zach, I'm hurt that you didn't tell her about me." He shot a mock glare at his friend. "I'm Jesse Calhoun. Call me Jesse or J.J., but make sure you call me."

Wiping off his hands with a towel, he reached out and enveloped hers in a handshake, giving her a slow exaggerated wink.

"What's the other J stand for?" she asked, ignoring his playfulness.

"His mother is inordinately proud of their family's cattle-thieving past, so she decided to name her only son Jesse James."

Zach reached over and pulled her hand out of Jesse's.

Jesse merely cocked an eyebrow at Zach before he moved

back toward the counter and continued trimming the steaks. Elizabeth saw the amused look on his face and wondered what he found so funny.

"Was your family related to Jesse James, then?" she asked.

She was curious about Jesse. Zach didn't let people close and she wanted to know more about him.

"Most of my family was quite divided after the Civil War. The side that lost went into cattle-thieving and bank robbing and the other half became Texas Rangers. My mama's family came mostly from the thieving side, so she's got a fondness for outlaws. Our family's reunions usually made the papers back then, between the fist fights and the occasional hangings."

His hearty laughter boomed throughout the kitchen, making Elizabeth smile. She could absolutely picture an all-out brawl between the different relatives of the Calhoun clan. Looking over her shoulder, she saw Zach smiling as well.

He let go of her once she was fully relaxed and moved into the kitchen. "What can I do to help?" she asked.

Zach pointed at a stool. "Sit."

"Okay," she said. She was a nightmare in the kitchen and had unintentionally used the smoke detectors in her apartment as timers in the past.

"Plus, I'm nearly done," Jessie said, grabbing some clean plates from the dishwasher.

Elizabeth asked, "Why do you live so far away from your family?"

"It's a long, tortured tale."

"He's the baby. And between his mother and six older, married, match-making sisters, he needed a place to hide."

Elizabeth shook her head a little. Zach still had the ability to cut right to the heart of the matter, tact be damned.

22

"I like my version better." Jesse clutched his heart and sighed.

"I think you're lucky to have family that cares." Elizabeth missed her mother more than she could say. And her father – she shied away from thinking about him. "What kind of business are you in? Zach doesn't tell me anything."

"You've been here all of ten hours and you slept most of that," Zach defended. "And you could use another eight to ten."

Elizabeth ignored him and turned her head toward Jesse. "As you were saying?"

"I like sassy women. You remind me of my sisters."

"That's really sweet."

Jesse shrugged and smiled.

"God, you're such a marshmallow." Zach said it so quietly that Elizabeth shot him a quick look. Wide-eyed, she checked to see how Jesse took it. When he smiled and gave Zach a shove, she guessed he wasn't bothered. Probably a guy thing.

"Why don't you tell Elizabeth exactly what we do," Jesse said.

Zach sat down and threw an arm around the back of Elizabeth's chair. Then he turned his attention to her. The force of his intensity hit her squarely in the stomach. Warmth spread through her body. She crossed her arms on the table in front of her chest. It was embarrassing…the way her body reacted to a simple look.

Jesse was just as good looking, but she felt nothing when he looked at her.

Zach's thumb caressed small circles on her back as Elizabeth waited for him to speak. "It's a security business."

"Like bodyguard stuff?"

"More like home and business security systems. Jess designs the systems, so they are unique to each business or home."

"Oh sure, tell her all the boring parts. Zach gets to have all the fun while I'm forced to work in the office all day. He gets to act like a burglar."

Elizabeth flinched at the wording, but tried not to show it. Zach frowned at Jesse, but when she shook her head, he didn't say anything. She thought she could guess what they were doing from some of Zach's cryptic letters. Not that he was ever intentionally cryptic, just not explanatory.

"So, Zach breaks into the home or business to assess the weak points and then you build a system to make sure he can't do it again without tripping the alarms. Is that right?"

Jesse smiled and saluted. "Sassy and smart. That's exactly right. He gets the adventure and I go blind programming the systems."

She liked the banter, even when Zach glared at his friend.

"I got the looks at least, and I laugh more often. He just makes grunting noises."

Elizabeth bit the inside of her cheek. Jesse's outrageous comments almost dragged another smile out of her. "You're so full of shit."

She was amazed at how comfortable she was with Jesse in the house. He was light and fun, where Zach was dark and serious; they complimented each other. They made her feel like she belonged. It was a rare experience and she savored it.

"I'm not an invalid," she muttered, as Zach shooed her into the living room after dinner.

"You are my guest," Zach said.

"Jesse's a guest too, and he's allowed to help."

"You can come over to my place tomorrow and cook and clean to your heart's content."

Zach moved from the kitchen to the living room, standing with his back to the fireplace. "Go home, Jess."

"Stop being rude to your friend," Elizabeth said.

"Zach's being more social than I thought he'd be, given

the circumstances. I need to get home anyway. It's a three mile hike to my place."

"You live that close?"

"Zach and I bought neighboring patches of land."

Jesse walked to the door. Elizabeth went to shake his hand. "It was really nice meeting you."

"You too. Don't let Zach scare you away. I'd like to see your pretty face again soon." Jesse reached out and, instead of shaking her hand, he enveloped her in a bear hug. When he let go, they were both grinning from ear to ear.

Then, Zach shoved him out the door.

CHAPTER 4

"Can we have a fire?"

"Sure."

Zach knelt by the fireplace, placing logs and kindling in a pyramid. When he struck the match and tossed it inside, the wood caught and blazed, casting his face in flickering shadows. Such a grim face. Elizabeth wished he would smile more. He was handsome, but when he actually smiled – then he took her breath away.

"What did you find out this afternoon? About the break-ins?"

The heat coming off the fire couldn't dispel the chill her question caused. She hated that she was still so freaked out, but couldn't stop the dread.

"What makes you think I know anything?"

"Because you are who you are."

Zach moved to the couch and sat on the floor, his back reclined against her knees. With a blanket over her arms and lap, and Zach's warm back against her legs, the frosty feeling of dismay that had been with her all week slowly gave way.

It was safe here.

As he stared into the flames, Zach rubbed his back against her. It was like a large bear trying to scratch an itch against a tree. Smiling, Elizabeth untangled her arms from the blanket and scratched the middle of his back. A rumbling grunt of approval reached her ears as he leaned his head forward and goose bumps spread over his skin.

"You have no idea how good that feels."

"Tell me about your phone calls," she asked, rubbing her palms up to his shoulders to work out the knot of tension he carried there. "Do they have any suspects yet?"

"No. They don't have any usable prints. The guy wore gloves and the DNA results aren't back yet. Those tests take time."

"I guess I hoped this was some random thing. Maybe a junkie with a criminal history, someone easily caught." Leaning forward, Elizabeth wrapped her arms around Zach's neck and nestled her head between his shoulder blades. "Why is this happening to me?"

Zach reached up and threaded his fingers through hers. His hands were big and warm and gave her a little tingle. "I don't know, but you're safe here. I won't let anything happen to you."

"I know."

It was so easy being with Zach. It always had been. If only he didn't want more than she could give him. More than she could give anyone.

"Did you leave because of me?"

"To the Marines?"

"Yes." Her voice caught. She was digging at an old wound, but like something infected, it needed to be ripped open and cleaned. It continued to cloud their relationship, making it strained. Even now, she felt it like a shadow, lurking in the back of their minds.

"I asked you to marry me, Beth. You can't even say the words."

There it was. Raw and angry. Even though his voice held no inflection. "We were too young."

"I knew what I wanted." He unthreaded his fingers from hers and moved away to shuffle the logs around in the fire.

The warmth moved away with him. She slumped back against the couch and ran a hand through her hair. "We could have still been together. You know I wanted that."

"That's just sex." He turned and speared her with a look. "I wanted more than that from you."

"You know how I feel about mar—commitment," she gulped. He was right, she couldn't even say the stupid word. "It's nothing but a trap. Look at the divorce rate in this country. It's more than fifty percent. It's old-fashioned and outdated."

"Well, I guess I'm old fashioned. I'm not your asshole father, Beth. And you sure as hell aren't your mother."

"Leave my mom out of this."

Zach frowned, but continued. "She's part of the reason you feel like this. You try to lay all the blame on how your dad treated you both, but the fact is, she could have left any time. She didn't. She stayed and kept you both in that hell."

She shied away from thinking about them. Better to focus on her and Zach. "You never answered the question. Is that why you left?"

"Partly."

She waited when he got quiet. The room was toasty warm now and the sun was setting. Finally, he looked her in the eyes and answered.

"I needed to get away from you. I could have taken the sex, but it wouldn't have been enough back then. And I was angry." He shrugged and shook his head. "I knew I needed discipline and I needed a sense of family. Foster care didn't give me either of those. The Marines gave me both."

"Everything I couldn't give you," she said, as she fought off the ridiculous need to cry. "I'm sorry."

"Don't be. You were right; we were too young."

He stood and smiled down at her while he stretched and she could tell that he was no longer willing to talk about it. At least she'd been brave enough to ask.

"Tell me about the next book."

She blinked away the moisture in her eyes and accepted the change of subject. "Did you actually read the first one?"

"Of course I did. Made the other guys buy copies too."

"Really?" She laughed at the thought of a bunch of bad-ass Special Ops guys reading her romance novels. "What did you think?" She looked up, wanting to see his expression.

"I love your imagination. The guys gave me a ration of shit over the sex scenes, but the Lieutenant sent it home to his wife and she's impatiently waiting for the next book. I promised you'd sign it for her."

Joy spread through her. Someone out there wanted to read her stuff. It was a heady feeling...And showed Zach still cared about her as a friend, not just someone he felt he needed to protect.

Elizabeth grinned and nodded. "Thank you, that was really sweet. And, of course, I'll sign it for her."

"I liked the sex scenes," he said, coming to sit next to her on the couch. "But they made me jealous as hell."

"Jealous of what?"

"Whoever inspired them. Those scenes—"

Elizabeth shook her head and laughed, letting out a tiny snort. "My imagination has been better than the real thing."

His incredulous look made her laugh again. "I think maybe I'm frigid."

"You're not."

"How do you know?"

"I just do."

"But how?" she asked.

"No one writes scenes as hot as yours without having passion inside of them. You've just never found the right man to ignite that fire."

The tips of her ears got hot. "How did we even get on this topic?" The blanket on her was suddenly stifling. But it made her feel good to think maybe she wasn't an ice queen.

"Why don't you go lie down and catch a nap? You could use more sleep."

"What about you? Is my stay going to be an inconvenience to someone?" She hadn't had the nerve to ask outright this morning when she arrived.

"You asking about my love life, Beth?"

"Seems only fair." Elizabeth laughed when he ignored her question and tugged her toward the back of the house and the bedrooms. "Well--?"

"There've been a few women here and there. Nothing serious."

The lead weight that had settled in her stomach lifted at his terse words. She hadn't realized she cared about that. It wasn't something she dwelled on, and yet, "Why nothing serious?"

"There are two kinds of women. The kind you marry and the ones you don't."

"And you pick the kind you don't?"

When he didn't answer, she realized they were standing in front of the master bedroom. "I can take the guest room, Zach. Thanks for letting me use your bed this morning."

"I'll take the guest bed. I'm up early and, this way, you can sleep in." He leaned down and gave her a chaste kiss on the forehead. "The dresser next to the bed is empty. You can put your stuff in there."

"Okay." Giving into to the impulse, she slid her arms around his neck and gave him a quick peck on the lips. When she pulled back, he looked stunned.

"Thanks for being there for me."

Stepping back, she shut the door.

THE WIND HOWLED through the trees and Elizabeth huddled under the covers. She'd been deeply asleep when the noise began. A low moan escaped as thunder crackled and then erupted into a house-shaking boom. Rain pelted the house like bullets, fast and furious.

She'd hated storms for as long as she could remember. It had everything to do with the night her parents died. It had been storming and her parents had been out to a movie. She'd begged her father to let her go to the school football game, but he didn't want her to leave home while he was gone—he never liked them out of his reach for long. So when they left, he'd locked Elizabeth's door from the outside, trapping her inside. Hours passed and he didn't let her out, not even when the storm rolled in and blew out the power across town.

She had pounded on the door, begging to be let out. It wasn't until the next day, when Zach and the police found her curled up on the floor by her bedroom door that she learned about the accident.

The hairs on her arms rose up as the static electricity in the room increased. A moment of silence and then the thunder lashed out so strong that the windows in the bedroom shuddered. Elizabeth swallowed the scream that crawled up her throat. Scooting backward, so that she was against the headboard, she pulled a pillow to her chest like a shield. It would be over soon.

Please, God, let it be over soon.

"Elizabeth?" His voice was a gift from heaven.

He stood by the door. No shirt, his blue jeans rode low on his hips and the top button was undone. He was so beautiful, standing there like some Roman statue come to life. Sculpted muscles, six pack abs and a light dusting of dark hair arrowed into a sexy little happy trail to the top of his jeans. She couldn't speak, couldn't tell him that she'd be okay, because her voice was trapped inside.

Lightning blazed across the sky and illuminated the room for a moment. She jumped and buried her face into the pillow. Half a second later, the bed dipped and strong arms wrapped around her body. Elizabeth abandoned the pillow, wound her arms around Zach's waist and held on for dear life.

"The nightmare again?"

A shaky, humorless laugh escaped. "You'd think it would have changed after all these years."

She rubbed her face against his hard chest and bit her lip to keep the hysteria at bay.

He hugged her closer. "This isn't supposed to last long."

The warmth Zach radiated from his body gradually worked its magic. Time meant nothing as he held her. The storm raged furiously as Elizabeth fought for control.

The storm didn't last as long as she feared it would, just like Zach promised. Gradually, the rain slowed to a gentle tip tap against the windows. The thunder moved away, until only distant echoes of sound reached her ears. Her death grip on Zach's waist loosened, but she wasn't ready to let go. Not when she felt so secure, so warm.

"I'm better now." Elizabeth blew out a sigh. "Thanks for remembering."

He smelled good. And with the smell of fresh rain and his own unique scent, she just wanted to bury her nose in his neck and sleep there. Even while the storm held her within its grip, her body responded to his. Her breasts felt full and heavy. Butterflies zinged back and forth across her stomach as he began to move away.

"You'll be able to sleep now. The storm has moved north."

Zach gave her one last hug and eased off the bed. She didn't want him to go. Didn't want him to walk away from her again. This was the moment. The moment she'd both dreaded and dreamed about.

God, she wanted him, wanted to prove to herself that she wasn't a frigid woman. But he'd rejected her once. Told her that what she had to offer wasn't enough.

"I don't want you to sleep in the other room, Zach. I want you to sleep here. With me."

His hand tightened on the doorknob, and he slowly shook his head. She could see the muscles of his back tense.

"Please don't say no. I need you."

He turned around and looked at her, hands fisted at his sides. The room lit up from another lightning flash; his blue eyes glowed in the light. His face was hard, but he didn't scare her.

"What are you asking for?"

"Make love to me, Zach."

CHAPTER 5

The king size bed swallowed her body. The lightning gave him glimpses of her blonde hair and huge eyes. The T-shirt she wore did little to hide her curves and his already overheated body went into overdrive.

"I want you," she said. Her tongue slipped out to moisten her lower lip. "I've wanted to see where this might go for a long time. I know you've thought about it too."

His gaze dropped to her tightly beaded nipples, outlined perfectly through the soft white cotton of the tee. "Is that the only thing you want, Beth? A quick lay, for old time's sake?"

"Yes," she said simply. "That's what I want."

She barely had the words out of her mouth when Zach moved. The breath he'd been holding rushed out as he stalked toward the bed. He sat on the edge and, when she reached for him, he pulled her onto his lap and buried his face into the crook of her neck, raining kisses on the exposed skin.

"Are you sure?"

But he didn't wait for her answer. Maybe he was afraid to hear more. And maybe he just needed to get out of his own head and take what she offered this time. No strings attached.

His mouth found hers in a scorching kiss. Her soft lips parted and he swept his tongue inside. She wrapped her arms around his neck and shifted her body closer, pressing her breasts against his chest. She tasted like peaches and honey.

Even sweeter than he ever imagined.

He stroked up her back, soothing the restless movements she made. With one hand tangled in her hair, the other reached down and cupped a full breast. His thumb caressed her in a tight circle, causing her breath to catch.

"You're so beautiful," Zach said, kissing her nose, her eyes, and returning to her lips.

He reached for the hem of her tee, slowly pulling the white cotton up until it was over her head, and then flung it to the side. She sat proudly, letting him look his fill.

"Like what you see, Marine?"

"So lovely," he groaned. "Even better than I'd imagined."

Laying her back against the pillows, he covered her with his body. She gripped his biceps and ran her hands over his shoulders to his back. Nails scraped against the nape of his neck and his body hardened almost to the point of pain.

Turning his attention to her rosy nipples, he took one into his mouth, nipping lightly. He heard her moan and felt her tremble, as he gave an equal amount of attention to the other. Her back arched as her fingers tunneled into his hair. The feel of her hands was a little piece of heaven, urging him to claim her.

But he needed to slow down or this show would be over too quickly.

Zach slipped between her thighs, nudging the bulge in his jeans against the heat of her. The sweet scent of her arousal engulfed him. He flexed his hips against her.

"Oh, God," Beth moaned. "That feels really good. But I

want more."

She stroked her hand down his firm stomach to the button that was undone. He turned so she could touch him. The hiss of his zipper as it went down made him pause and groan as his erection sprang free of the tight confines.

Beth palmed him, before giving a squeeze. She rubbed up and down his length giving him so much pleasure he was ready to go off in her hand like a teenager.

"I want to see all of you," she said.

"I aim to please." Zach left her to slide his jeans off and kick them across the room, drinking in the sight of her flushed body the whole time. Her eyes raked him from head to toe as he stood there. The hunger on her face matched his own.

Zach bent over and hooked his thumbs under the white string edges of the sexy lace underwear and slowly pulled it off. "My turn."

He pulled her up by her hands and ordered, "Kiss me again."

◌◌

ELIZABETH TOOK HER TIME, running her hands over his thickly-muscled chest and arms. He was so hard and such a contrast to her soft body. Darkly tanned from time spent out of doors, it was a thrilling little shock to see her pale hand up against his darker skin.

She smiled and reached up to give him a lingering kiss. "I've wanted this for a long time, Zach."

He chuckled lightly. "I won't lie, I've thought about this myself. More than I want to admit."

"You always were stubborn."

With his tongue and lips, he blazed a trail of heat from her neck down to her stomach. He kissed his way past her belly button and blew gently on the blonde hair shielding the bundle of nerves that craved his attention.

The cooler air made her whole body vibrate and tingle, but before she could catch her breath, she felt his tongue. Zach licked her in one long, deliberate swipe, wrenching a moan out of her.

"Oh, yes," she panted, gripping the bedspread.

Her thighs opened wider in invitation as she felt his fingers start to explore. Zach's dark head between her creamy thighs was such an erotic sight that her entire body tensed with need. Never in her entire life had she wanted a man as much as she wanted him.

Her body was molten lava under Zach's touch. It was a revelation.

One finger entered her and she was dizzy with pleasure. But when his mouth covered her and began sucking and licking, she just let go and moaned...long and loud.

"God, you taste good."

"I need more," she said, mindlessly lifting her hips. She was almost there. Almost over the edge with pleasure. He gave one last lick and crawled back up her body to take her mouth. She tasted herself on his tongue, tangy and sweet.

He moved to the side to open the top drawer of the night-stand and grab a condom. Donning the latex, he nipped her neck and then he whispered, "Wrap your legs around me."

Heat licked across her skin consuming her as she felt him slowly penetrate her. Her legs were up around his middle as inch-by-glorious-inch, he pushed into her, stretching her. He rocked in and out, going in further and farther with each thrust.

Elizabeth gasped as he thrust hard one more time and

was seated to the hilt. He held still then, letting her adjust to his size. His breathing was hard and his body was tense. She loved his control and strength.

"How does that feel?"

"It'd feel better if you *moved*," she said, straining closer. Her arms locked around his neck as he teased her with long, drugging kisses.

"I want to make this good for you."

"It's already better than anything I've ever experienced," she whispered. When she felt him stop, she worried that her words were a turn off. Who wanted a woman everyone else said was frigid?

"Jesus," he said in a strangled voice, looking deep into her eyes. "I'll make sure it's the best. Hold on." Then he exploded in movement, rocking in and out of her harder, and faster. "Is this what you want?"

Her head thrashed back and forth on the pillow, "Yes, oh yes."

The pleasure was so intense, she worried she would fly apart. Her thighs trembled as she held on.

How often had she dreamed of this? Zach loving her, pleasuring her, making her his for the night. He sat up on his knees and hooked her legs over his forearms, still thrusting into her. And when he used his thumbs on her, the world tilted. She convulsed around him, her orgasm harder and better than anything she'd ever done herself.

"Look at me," he demanded. When her eyes found his, he thrust harder, watching her every movement. "Who's in your bed, Beth? In your body?"

"You are," she rasped. Elizabeth's orgasm still rolled through her, wrenching another moan out of her.

Zach's breath hissed through clenched teeth as he ground his hips against her, drawing out her pleasure as he found his.

"Oh. My. God...Zaaaccchhh!"

Releasing her legs, he collapsed with a groan, landing on his elbows, on either side of her head. He kissed her closed eyes and then moved to her lips, kissing her over and over as he gathered her into his arms and slid them both under the covers.

She curled into his side and threw an arm across his chest.

"That was way better than anything I've ever written about."

"Yes, ma'am. It sure was."

She grinned, "You've been spending too much time with Jesse. He's rubbing off on you."

A swat on her fanny turned the grin into a laugh before she got a kiss on the head and an aggravated, "Stop thinking about my best friend."

"You sound a little nervous. Afraid I will try and seduce your buddy now that I've had a taste of the good stuff?"

Zach shook his head and closed his eyes. "Go to sleep."

She didn't want to sleep. She wanted to talk about the amazing thing that just happened between them. But Zach was right. He'd been up at Lord knows what hour this morning and then he'd come to her rescue during the storm.

And then there was the sex. Her steamy novels were about to hit a whole new level.

Elizabeth yawned, warm and content. When he growled sleepily and pulled her closer, she tried to keep still. Her last thought was filled with satisfaction.

She *definitely* wasn't frigid.

⬜⬜

THE RAIN KEPT the nosy people inside their homes, huddled under the covers. That suited the secret admirer just fine. He was up the tree and at her apartment window in no time. He popped the screen and set it safely into the groove he'd notched into the bark of the branch he was on. Then he used a screwdriver to jimmy open Elizabeth's window.

It took him less than three minutes.

Everyone underestimated his strength and ingenuity. Even his own family, but that was fine with him. Being thought of as inferior gave him the kind of camouflage he needed to go about his business.

The apartment smelled like her. That's what he liked about Elizabeth, that she was clean and pure. Not like the others. Fucking sluts out to take everything they could from a man.

But not his Elizabeth. She was special.

Taking out his pen light, he swept it around the bedroom. She still wasn't home, but she would come back. And when she did, she would find his gift. A little token to show his affection. An apology, of sorts, about the mess.

Humming a little tune, he moved around the room, cleaning and placing everything back the way she liked it. He pulled out the pictures he had of the bedroom. It had to be perfect.

He hadn't meant to scare her, but he'd been angry and confused that she hadn't been home to greet him the last time. He'd planned everything down to the last detail, but she hadn't come home at her normal time. That's another reason he planted the camera. He wanted to be prepared next time.

But that was in the past. She would come back and she would be overjoyed by his surprise.

Then she would give herself to him. In all the ways he imagined.

CHAPTER 6

*E*lizabeth followed her nose to the kitchen and found hot coffee waiting after waking alone. Pouring a cup, she leaned back against the counter and took her time looking around. She loved that the kitchen and living area were one big open room. The ceiling was high and huge windows showcased the beauty of the forest landscape outside.

Zach craved large amounts of light and space, neither of which he'd had at the foster home. He'd created a beautiful home, made to fit his size and needs. He was an amazing man. And boy oh boy, did Zach know what he was doing in the bedroom. There wasn't a part of her body that he hadn't touched, licked or kissed. She smelled like sex and Zach.

Zach strolled in through the patio doors carrying a load of firewood. He hadn't seen her behind the counter yet and she used that moment to watch him. Moving silently, his dark green thermal shirt molded to his muscular chest and traced the lines of his biceps. And when he bent down to unload the firewood, faded blue jeans cupped an ass that made her mouth water.

Elizabeth stifled a moan but must have made some kind of noise, because she watched Zach's shoulders tense and then relax again. He finished what he was doing and then stood, turning those deep blue eyes on her.

"Did you get enough sleep?" he asked.

Elizabeth set her mug on the counter. "You were there. Do you think I got enough sleep?"

He was the only person in the world that she felt like she could be herself around.

"I think you need more. Maybe you should go back to bed."

"Only if you come with me."

She couldn't believe that popped out of her mouth. Did they have support groups for sex-starved writers? Elizabeth didn't know, but she wasn't sure she would ever be able to get enough of Zach. Once was not going to be enough for her.

She watched with interest as he prowled around the over-stuffed couch toward her. "I have work to do."

"What kind of work?"

"Jesse and I have a client to meet today at noon. I want you here, where I know you're safe, and I want you to rest."

"I'd rather we both went back to bed."

Instead of answering her, Zach leaned in close and gave her a long, slow kiss that curled her toes.

"Good morning, Beth."

"Good morning, Zach."

It shouldn't be legal what the man did to her. Used to being an independent person, Zach's kisses made her a slave to his taste.

"I need to shower and get ready for the meeting. I'll make you something for breakfast before I go."

Elizabeth stood there only half-hearing what he said. She hated that he was so composed, while she felt out of control about last night. Just once, she would like to catch him off-guard and crack that composure.

"No, I'm fine. Go get ready and I'll fix a small breakfast for myself. I've been taking care of myself for a while now. What's in the locked room?"

"Some dream I used to have." He shrugged and didn't say anything more.

Elizabeth tried to gave him a shove. He didn't even budge, merely lifted an eyebrow. He knew how much she hated secrets. And locked doors. Hated even more being told how to feel or act. And even if this was his house, it pissed her off.

She didn't have experience sharing space with men, but she knew Zach. It wouldn't be his intent to make her angry. And sex didn't need to change everything. She didn't want to lose her best friend over *her* childhood issues.

Taking a deep breath, she smiled and let go of her issues. At least for a moment.

◻◻

THE STUBBORN TILT to Beth's chin wasn't the only evidence of the temper lurking underneath the stillness. Fire flashed in her eyes when she'd tried to shove him. Planting a quick kiss to her pert nose, he left her fuming in the hall and went to take a shower.

A cold shower.

Zach wasn't a fool, but he'd made a tactical error in giving in to her and his own raging lust. When he was younger, he'd wanted everything from Beth, not just her body. He'd wanted her mind, her soul, and her heart. He'd left when it was clear she wasn't willing to even entertain his marriage proposal. She'd hurt him by turning him down.

Now that she was here, he was having a hard time keeping things light. Especially after last night.

The primitive caveman that lurked inside of him smiled when he'd woken up with her in his arms. It demanded that he keep his woman, no matter what she had to say about it. The more enlightened side knew he was going to have to battle her history to win her.

Not to mention whoever was stalking her now.

And just like that, he was in over his head. Again. One night with her, that's what he'd told himself. Granted, it was a night he'd fantasized about for most of his adult life. But that was all it took to make him realize that he'd never really gotten over her. Never completely hardened his heart against her.

Shit, he still loved her.

He didn't shy away from the truth. And it didn't matter that so much time had passed. And he knew why he'd never taken any other women seriously. Beth was his whole heart; there just wasn't room for anyone else. Never would be.

He finished his shower and dried off, berating himself for letting himself get distracted. Today was about the job, but his gaze strayed to the bed.

Beth had been incredibly responsive to his touch. His body hardened at the memory. This client was the biggest one they'd ever had, otherwise he'd be tempted to blow off the meeting and take Beth back to bed.

Maybe stay there for the rest of his life.

Instead, he changed into black fatigue pants, a black T-shirt and black hiking boots. His burglar outfit. He'd be breaking into a warehouse with some fairly decent surveillance equipment. Nothing like Jesse could build, but Zach was always prepared.

When he left the room, he found Beth standing at the back door, looking outside. Her shoulders were taut and her sexy mouth was a thin line. She looked like she had the weight of the world on her shoulders.

"I have to head out," he said.

Beth jumped and let out a little squeak. Eyes wide, she turned to face him. "Sorry, I was miles away."

The fact that she relaxed immediately sent satisfaction through him. It pleased the hell out of him that she felt safe here with him. The evidence was there in her eyes and the ready smile that meant everything to him.

"When will you be back?"

Her face and that smile had gotten him through some tough times in even tougher countries while he was in the service. He could admit that now.

"It'll probably be several hours, but I'll be back as quickly as I can. Try not to burn the house down."

Beth laughed and that was the response he wanted. She'd always been such a serious little thing. He liked that she'd learned to smile and laugh. Besides, he was serious enough for both of them.

"I wouldn't dare."

Because he couldn't be close without touching her, he reached out and laced his fingers through hers. "Come with me. I want to show you how to use the alarm system."

"Don't worry so much. I'm not planning on moving from the couch until you get back."

At the alarm panel, Zach showed Beth how to punch in the code to arm and disarm the system. When he was satisfied that she was comfortable with the codes, he turned her around and pressed her back against the wall. He leaned down and pressed his mouth to hers.

Beth's lips parted on a sigh and he used that opening to tangle his tongue with hers. She tasted like coffee and cream and a goodness that lightened his soul. Running his hands around her ribcage, he smoothed down her back and cupped her ass. A perfect fit for his hands, everything about this woman fit and completed him.

"Don't go," she whispered.

Damn, but he wished he could stay. "I have to."

"Well, if you promise to pick up where you're leaving off..."

Zach smiled. Beth trying to be bold was cute. "I want you to think about something today. Something serious."

Chocolate brown eyes gazed into his with an expression of trust so beautiful that he almost didn't say anything more. He knew how his question would hit her, but he needed it to be out in the open. The more time she had to think, the better his chances of having her in his life would be.

"What is it?"

"I want more, Beth. More of you, me, this. Think about staying here for the summer and giving this a real chance." He'd bring up marriage and kids later.

Her faced paled instantly and she pulled her hand away from his. "W-what?" Beth sucked a breath and held it, clenching and unclenching her hands. "I thought we were clear about what this is."

Zach could feel his jaw clench. "I thought we were clear too. I wanted it to just be sex, Beth. But it's not. It never has been with you and me and I can't pretend that it is. So at the risk of having my pride and my heart stomped on—again— I'm asking you to think about it."

"You know I can't stay. I have a book to write, a life in Phoenix. I can't just put it all on hold."

"I'm asking you to give me a few months, see where this goes. Not put your life on hold. We belong together. I've known it our whole lives, and, if you'd let yourself, you'd see it too."

"Zach—"

"Just think about it. That's all I'm asking." He kissed her quickly on the lips and then opened the door. "Set the alarm. I'll be back soon."

Then he left and prayed that she had the courage to start thinking past her fear of commitment. This was his only shot at a normal life with the woman he loved. It was Beth or a life alone, but he was willing to take the chance. He just hoped to God that he could convince her.

CHAPTER 7

*E*lizabeth set the alarm and walked on wooden legs to the couch. Sinking down onto the leather, she pulled her knees to her chest and wrapped her arms around them. Move in? He wanted to live together for the summer? What was he thinking?

Chills raced down her arms and nausea rolled through her empty stomach. The only thing that kept her rooted to the spot and not running for the hills was Zach. Big, sexy, irritating, incredible Zach. Her bastion against the world.

But what he was asking was something more permanent.

That kind of life wasn't for her. That led to emotions, entanglements, commitment, all of which lead to marriage. She still had nightmares from her so-called family life, before the crash. Marriage was unstable. Better to be single and able to walk out at any time, before everyone involved got hurt.

And what about children? That came with marriage.

He deserved kids. Zach would be a wonderfully loving and patient father, but she wasn't even sure she would know what to do with a child. She'd never been one herself. Growing up, she had to be quiet for Daddy, because he didn't like noise. No running and playing like a normal kid. She had to dress a certain way and was only allowed to speak when asked a question. She and her mother could only eat after he'd eaten.

Her mother said marriage was forever – for better or worse. It was marriage and a child that kept her mother in that hell. If it hadn't been for her, Elizabeth believed her mother might have left, instead of settling for a life of submissive servitude.

All she knew for certain was that her father had killed her mother. Oh, not literally. A drunk driver had done that for both of them, but he'd killed her spirit long before her body had died.

No man would ever be able to have a say in her life like her father had. Somewhere, deep down, she'd thought Zach understood that. Understood that sex was just that—sex— with no agenda.

She needed some air.

She turned off the alarm so she could step out onto the back porch, a gentle breeze caressed her face. She inhaled strongly, closing her eyes to savor the scent and the calm that washed over her. Then she shoved the anxiety out of her head. At least for now.

Not wanting to go far, but eager to focus on something else, she stepped off the back porch for a better look at the house. An enormous bay window caught her attention. Excited with her discovery, Elizabeth made her way over to the window to snoop.

"Damn!" The entire window was covered from the inside.

She jumped when her cell phone buzzed. She'd forgotten that it was in her back pocket. Gingerly extracting the device, the caller ID said "Unknown." She answered anyway.

"Hello?"

"Ms. Russell? It's Detective Wolfe, do you have a minute?"

"Sure, Detective, and please, call me Elizabeth."

"Alright, Elizabeth. I was calling to give you an update. Unfortunately, I don't have any new information or suspects yet, but I wanted you to know that we've released your apartment. The crime lab has processed everything they need for the investigation, so you're welcome to come home at any time."

"That's good news." Elizabeth tried to muster up some enthusiasm, but just couldn't face the prospect of her ravaged apartment.

"It's really only a matter of time before we catch this guy. I'll make sure of it," he said, confidence radiating through the line. "If you like, I can meet you and escort you home. I understand it's unsettling to go in alone for the first time."

"That's very kind of you Detective, but—"

"I'd like it if you called me Daniel," he interrupted. "Unofficially, of course."

"Thank you, Daniel, but I'm actually with a friend. He's helping me out and letting me stay until this whole thing is resolved."

There was a long pause and then, "You never mentioned him in the report. Maybe I should interview him."

"He isn't involved. Believe me." Elizabeth felt guilty about not mentioning Zach to the detective before. "I *am* glad you called, though. I appreciate the offer, but I don't think I'll come back until this over."

"That's understandable. I do need an inventory of items missing and I need to get your signature for the victim statement." His voice had subtly changed into a more professional tone.

"Is that something that needs to be done immediately?"

"Why don't you give me the address of where you're staying and I'll drop off the forms."

"Okay." She gave the address and Zach's name.

"Flagstaff, huh? I guess I won't be stopping by to give you the forms then. I'll stick them in the mail for you. Just make sure you get them back as soon as you can."

"No problem. Sorry for not telling you where I went; it was a last minute decision. I feel safer here. Stupid, I guess."

"Not at all. And it's only natural to want distance between yourself and the violence you've experienced."

"I appreciate the understanding."

"I'll be in touch. You have my card with you?"

"Yes."

"My cell and home numbers are on the back. If you need anything, or just want to talk, call me. Anytime."

〇〇

ZACH WAS on his way back home from the meeting when his phone rang. Seeing Jesse's number, he answered, thinking it was something to do with the business.

"What's up?"

"Got some news from one of my sources. It's not good."

"Just spit it out."

"Well, Detective Wolfe has an interesting past. And a tie to your girl."

Zach could feel his teeth clench as he stepped on the accelerator. Damn it, he knew he should've blown off the meeting and just let Jesse handle the clients.

"He was the first officer on the scene at the accident that killed Beth's parents and he's from Casa Grande. He moved to Phoenix about three years ago and moved up to Detective with Phoenix PD."

"Why don't I know him?"

"He's at least five years older. You probably wouldn't have crossed paths."

"It's not a big town, Jess. And now he's in the middle of another case involving Beth. That's one helluva coincidence."

"You don't believe in coincidences," Jesse reminded him.

"Damn it, I know. You got anything else on this guy?"

"Not yet, but I'm still digging. I don't have anything on the other names you gave me yet either."

"Let me know when you do. This bastard is clever."

Zach hung up and pushed his truck faster. He needed to see Beth and make sure she was exactly how he left her. And if even a single hair was out of place, there would be hell to pay.

He pulled up to the house and was up to the steps when he froze.

Singing.

Beth was singing. Outside. Alone.

Zach was pissed. Finding Beth outside made his skin crawl. He'd only left the house because he was sure she'd be safe and he'd be notified immediately if one of the alarms was tripped. But not if the damned woman disarmed them herself.

He rounded the corner at the back of the house and there she was, sitting in the sun as if she hadn't a care in the world.

"What the hell are you doing?"

"Zach. I didn't realize you were home."

"Because you should be inside sitting innocently on the couch."

If steam could actually shoot out of a person's ears, Zach was mad enough to make it happen. Didn't she realize that anything could have happened? Her stalker could have easily attacked her. More than anything, he was angry that he'd left her at all. It wouldn't happen in the future.

"I-I'm sorry." Beth took a deep breath and then that stubborn chin lifted a notch. "Damn it, no, I'm not. I'm not a prisoner here. Stop acting like I am."

He advanced on her, making her back up a step. "You are not a prisoner here. But you put me in charge of your safety."

He let his eyes roam the curves that his hands had explored. The fire in her eyes only stroked his need. Zach's body stirred, overriding his anger.

"It's safe here, Zach. And I wanted to be outside for a few minutes to clear my mind and get some fresh air. Jesus, I'm on the porch."

Knowing he was scaring her a little, he took a deep breath and willed his calm to return. It wasn't her fault that someone had targeted her. And she didn't have the new information that he had.

"It's not as safe as you think."

"You're pissed because you told me not to leave the house and I did."

And that was something her father would have done. Zach wasn't winning any points here and he knew it, but he couldn't necessarily control his possessive personality either.

He sighed and shook his head.

"There are bears up here in the mountains, you know." He was under control again and he was sorry he yelled. But the thought of anything happening to her, well, he didn't even want to think about it.

"You're the only grumpy bear around right now," she said, crossing her arms and glaring at him. It was her tough look, one she'd perfected in high school.

He towered over her when he stood close. The smell of the peaches and cream scent that clung to her skin reached him, calming him further.

"You know what happens when you poke a bear?"

"He grunts and grumbles and growls like he's got a thorn

in his paw?" She shrugged. "Who can know with bears? I hear they're stubborn."

Zach growled low in his throat and snaked his arms around her body to cup her ass. Up close, her feminine scent created an instant response. He could be ninety and half dead and she could still get him to respond to her.

"They take what they want, when they want it."

She stood rigid in his arms, refusing to look up at him.

"I'm sorry, Beth."

Beth toyed with the hair at the nape of his neck. It took her a few minutes, but gradually, she forgave him for being hotheaded. Her eyes softened and she lightly dragged her nails against his scalp.

"Tell me more," she whispered into his ear.

He moved closer, feeling her soft body yield to his stronger one. It would be so easy to pick her up and take her back to bed. Satisfaction guaranteed, for both of them. But that wasn't going to happen. He needed to focus and keep his mind on the prize: Beth's heart, not just her gorgeous body.

And the first step was getting her over the irrational fear of living together and her instant reactions to anything that sounded like a command from him.

"Did you think about what I said?"

Her restless fingers stilled in his hair. "Why can't we just stay in the moment? Why does this have to be defined?"

Zach hugged Beth close, trying his best to comfort her and ignore his body demanding he have his way with her. He was not sympathetic to her plight, however; this was about both of them, not just her past.

If she walked away from him, it wasn't going to be pretty.

"Living together makes sense, Beth, for both of us. We could be with each other all the time, in all the ways your father never let us. The sex is great. Hell, it would even be better for tax purposes."

The tax thing was spur of the moment, but she laughed a little when he said it, just like he hoped she would. Beth was terrified of love and marriage. Taxes were a universal fear and, as irrational as it was, she was more comfortable with that than love.

"Like a business arrangement?" She pulled back and narrowed her eyes. "No mushy emotional entanglements?" Biting her lower lip, she dropped her eyes and then her hands. "What about kids?"

"We handle whatever comes our way, together."

"I just don't know. You know how I feel about commitment. What if I can't do it?"

"You're the only woman I will ever be with like this, Beth. If you say no, I'll live and die alone."

She looked into his eyes for a long moment, maybe searching for the truth or hoping that deep down he was kidding. But he wasn't. It was her or no one.

"Who can resist the allure of sticking it to the IRS?" she said after a couple of moments.

It wasn't the answer he wanted, but at least she wasn't running away either. It was a start. Something to build on. He wouldn't stop trying until she finally agreed to be his wife.

CHAPTER 8

*E*lizabeth hugged Zach, knowing that he was only trying to ease her fear by suggesting this so-called business arrangement. It was sweet and the least romantic thing someone could possibly say while talking about moving in together. But coming from Zach, it was beautiful.

She would think about it, even if it terrified her. She owed it to him to at least consider it. The last time he'd suggested anything like this was when he'd proposed to her. She'd been seventeen and finally free after her father's death. She'd hurt Zach deeply by her instant refusal back then, but there was no way she was willing to even dwell on the possibility of binding herself to someone.

"Let's go back inside and have some lunch. I'm starving," he said, tugging her up the steps.

Elizabeth couldn't help her instant relief at the change in topic. "Can we go into Flagstaff for lunch and a bit of shopping?"

His brow furrowed a bit. "What do you need in town?"

"Clothes and girl stuff." She held back her smile when Zach immediately grabbed his keys. Girl stuff was as mysterious as a woman's purse. He was a guy and guys were terrified of lengthy explanations regarding feminine needs.

"Got it."

The ride into town was wild and a lesson in white-knuckle dashboard clutching. Zach drove an older model truck with a lift. She liked him cupping her ass to get her up into the cab. Otherwise, she'd have needed a step stool. And once they hit the main road, it was nice being up so high.

Zach told her that Flagstaff was still growing and was home to the Northern Arizona University Lumberjacks. It looked like an old west boom town mixed with newer, more modern architecture. Small Mom and Pop businesses were squashed up against each other with old-fashioned shingles out advertising the names of the businesses and old west facades sported new paint. Then, on the next block, a strip mall offered chain fast food restaurants and stores.

It was late afternoon and the streets were filled with people going about their day and throngs of college students who packed up their cars with bags of laundry and backpacks. Probably heading down the hill to Phoenix for the weekend.

Zach found a spot to park on historic Santa Fe Avenue and came around to open Elizabeth's door. He reached up and grabbed her around the waist, slowly dragging her from her seat.

Zach still had her suspended above the pavement when he leaned in and began nibbling on her lips. She wound her arms around his neck and, when she sighed, he took that opening to kiss her thoroughly.

Her eyes drifted closed and her world narrowed to Zach and his kiss. Her nipples hardened into points against his chest and her last pair of clean panties got wet.

"Maybe we should just go back home," Zach said.

"Maybe you should put me down and let me shop. And I'm pretty sure those guys over there are staring."

"Let them."

Zach brushed his lips gently against her nose and set her on her feet. That's when she noticed they were parked in front of the freshly-remodeled façade of one of the older buildings on the street. The window was ornately designed and boasted the name J.Z. Alarms and Consultation.

"Well, that's one way to attract business," Jesse said as he came through the door.

"Shut up, Jess," Zach said. "You're embarrassing Beth."

"Oh, *I'm* embarrassing Beth. I'm sure it had nothing to do with you mauling her on the front steps of the store." Jesse chuckled and winked.

"Hi, Jesse," Elizabeth said, emerging from Zach's embrace.

"Hey yourself. It's been too long since I've seen your beautiful face. Come on in and let me show you around our baby."

"The location is fabulous. I love how it looks fresh from the 1800s." She allowed Jesse to sweep his arm around her and lead her inside. When she glanced over her shoulder, Zach was scanning the street while he locked up his truck. He shot a glare at the guys who'd been staring and got a bunch of thumbs-ups before they turned back to loading a keg.

⬚⬚

"WHAT'S GOING on with the investigation?" Jesse asked Zach an hour later.

Zach stared out the front window as Beth walked into a

dress shop across the street. He hadn't wanted her going out by herself, but he also didn't want to smother her. She may not think she was in danger here, but Zach wasn't taking any chances. If she moved out of sight, he was ready to leave the store and follow along.

"They have a few leads, but Detective Wolfe has closed ranks and is keeping everything under wraps. Our conversation was less than pleasant. I'm not worried though; Little Mike's got friends in that office, so I'll know what he knows."

"Wow, Little Mike's a cop now? He'll either make Chief or end up in jail," Jesse said. "When did he get out? I lost track of him when he got orders for Bagdad."

"He's been out for a couple years now."

Zach knew Mike wouldn't let him down. He was a bulldog when he had an assignment.

"When are you going to marry her?"

"As soon as I can find a preacher willing to perform a ceremony with a handcuffed and gagged bride," Zach replied grimly.

"Gun shy, huh? Well, maybe she's looking for someone with a gentle nature and better cooking skills?"

Zach didn't bother to look at Jesse, just kept an eye on the street for anything suspicious. Beth hadn't left the dress shop yet. "You're my best friend, but I will kill you if you even think about it."

Jesse let out a loud laugh and walked up beside Zach. "She's something special, but I don't envy you," he said in a quiet tone. "She's jumpy as hell. It's obvious that she's got baggage. Are you sure she's what you want?"

"I've been sure since I was eighteen years old." Zach's tone was final. There was no hesitation. No doubt. She was his to love and cherish and she always would be. Even if she never married him.

"Does she love you?"

"Yeah, but she's going to fight me on it." Zach relaxed his stance. He'd never been a talker, but Jesse was his closest friend and would never betray his trust. "She doesn't like to talk about her home life. She'd kill me if she found out I'm telling you, but I have a clear picture of her past and why she shies away from just about anyone but me."

"Sounds bad."

"You have no idea." Zach closed his eyes for a moment, thinking about the sad little girl Beth had been. It had taken months before she would speak a single word to him. She'd been a freshman in high school and he'd begun sitting with her at lunch, just to try and get a response out of her. Something about her pulled at him, even in the beginning. She wouldn't even smile at him for the first year.

"I followed her home one day after school, trying to figure out what was going on. It was spring and the house was wide open, so I just sat in the bushes by the back door, listening. Didn't take long to understand why she hates even the thought of commitment."

Beth stepped out of the shop and walked to the next one. She stood there staring into the windows, looking lovely enough to break his heart. She wore low-rise blue jeans and a silky emerald-green tank top that showed off glimpses of creamy skin between the jeans and the top when she moved. Her long blonde hair hung loose around her shoulders, shining brightly in the sun.

"What happened to her?" Jesse asked.

"Her father was a son of a bitch. I don't think he was physically abusive, and if he was, it was toward her mother only. But he was emotionally intimidating and controlling. Told them when they could speak, when they could eat, and what they could wear. And her mother just went along with it. If Beth argued, then she was demeaned in the worst way."

Zach shook his head and had to unclench his fists. To this

day, he wished he could have found a way to get her out of that house sooner. But they'd both been kids.

"He used to lock Beth in her room if he thought she was getting smart with him. She wasn't allowed to go anywhere but school and home. She couldn't watch TV or have a radio, nothing but schoolwork and recreational reading from the Bible. No school events and, certainly, no dating."

"That's crazy," Jesse said.

"She has nightmares about him. She told me that, from the time she hit high school, her father was convinced that she was going to turn into a whore. He nailed her windows shut and locked her inside at night to make sure she couldn't sneak out. Beth was so traumatized by that bastard that she wouldn't even look at anyone at school or talk to them. I know she thinks she's a coward for not standing up to him, but she's got more strength than she realizes."

Zach reached up and rubbed the tension from his neck, flexing his shoulders. "She's terrified of marriage and kids. I think she's afraid history could repeat itself."

"So what's your plan of attack?" Jesse asked.

"I've got her thinking about moving in with me now. But I'm going to convince her to marry me, that I'm not going to start controlling her like her father did, and that we're meant for each other," Zach said with a shrug. "I figure if I keep her busy, happy and in bed for the next fifty or sixty years, by the time she knows what hit her, she'll be too old to leave me."

Jesse's laugh wrung a wry smile out of him. He wasn't convinced either, but he had to try.

"That's a helluva plan, my friend."

"I am adapting, improvising and overcoming."

"Ooh rah," Jesse finished.

61

"Did you get everything you wanted?"

Elizabeth nodded. "I loved the little boutiques and I was surprised that none of them were overly expensive."

"Flagstaff is a great town."

"Detective Wolfe called earlier. I forgot to tell you."

Zach looked over at her as he drove them home. The sun was setting and streaks of orange and pink lit the sky. Jesse had treated them both to lunch and dinner in town and she was full and happy with the quiet ride and gorgeous sunset.

"What did he say?" he asked.

"That I could go home."

The only sign that Zach even heard her was his hand tightening on the steering wheel. A tick started in his jaw, but he didn't say anything. She hadn't wanted to spoil the fun today with this.

"I told him that I didn't want to return until they had the suspect in custody. I wouldn't feel safe otherwise."

"You'll always be safe with me."

She sighed. "I know, but that isn't my problem and you know it."

"I think it is. Deep down, you're afraid to trust anyone."

"But I trust you."

Zach shook his head. "You trust me with your safety and with your body, but you don't trust me enough to give me anything else."

She knew he was talking about more than just moving in together. They were essentially living together now, at least in the short term. He was talking about much scarier things than co-habitation, and she was trying to be honest about her feelings.

"Marriage isn't exactly a great thing these days. The divorce rate is more than fifty percent."

"Those people aren't us."

She ran a shaky hand through her hair. He was so stubborn when he set his mind to something. It made her crazy. He made her crazy.

"Isn't there someone else you can marry?" she huffed out...and immediately knew it was the wrong thing to say. She didn't even mean it, not really. It was just her fear of commitment talking. It's not like she didn't know she had a phobia about it.

Zach threw her a disgusted look and didn't bother to answer.

Her cell phone rang at that moment, breaking some of the tension. Zach parked his truck as she answered.

"Hello?"

Nothing but silence.

"Hello? Is someone there?"

When still nothing was said, she disconnected the call and slid her phone back into her purse. She shrugged at Zach. "Must have been a wrong number."

"We're not done talking about this."

"Can we table it until later? Maybe after I have a hot shower and more sleep?"

Zach stared at her in the waning light. The man was sexy, whether he was frowning or smiling. It wasn't fair. She saw when he gave in and, even though it was a small reprieve, she was grateful.

Zach took all her bags into the house. While she went into the bedroom to put her stuff away and shower, he went through the house setting the alarms and making sure all the windows and doors were secure.

"Feel better?" he asked, watching her from the bed.

Elizabeth nodded, allowing her gaze to roam his body. His lightly furred chest gave way to lean hips. He had long muscular legs and, when she paused on his briefs, she noticed they were tented with his impressive erection.

Instant need ripped through her. He was her own personal drug and she wanted to show him how much he meant to her, even if she couldn't say the words. She was so good with words when she was writing, but when it came to speaking them out loud—she clammed up.

Stopping just short of the bed, Elizabeth finally tore her gaze from his length and looked into his hooded eyes. Very slowly, she brought her hands up to the knot in the towel, watching Zach's breathing change.

She loved that she affected him just as much as he affected her. He intoxicated her senses until she was deaf and blind to anything but him. She let the towel drop to the floor, baring herself to the only man who made her feel good just by looking at her. The cooler air on her nipples made them tighten. His mouth would warm them up nicely, but that would have to wait. She had other plans for the moment.

"You're going to kill me," he said in a strangled whisper. He shifted on the bed and reached an arm out to her.

"No. Not yet." She held her hand up, palm out, stopping his motions. "I want you to stay on the bed and take those off."

Zach's lips twitched as he took his briefs off, but he didn't laugh at her.

"I wanted to see all of you."

"And I want to taste all of you. Once wasn't enough."

She laughed, low and husky. "You can taste me after."

"After what?"

"After some torment and only if you're a good boy and do nothing but watch."

Zach was used to being in charge, but she wanted to see how far he'd let her go before he took over. In this one area, she wasn't afraid of his control. In fact, she liked it.

Elizabeth ran her hands slowly up her body cupping her breasts, kneading them lightly and squeezing her nipples between thumb and forefinger. She closed her eyes at the pleasure and sighed.

Making Zach watch was incredible foreplay.

Zach's breathing became harsh, the sound causing Elizabeth's eyes to snap open. She felt his desire. His thick sex jutted proudly, curving slightly and growing in size under her heated look.

"Sit up. I want you on the edge of the bed."

"Getting bossy. I like it."

He grinned as he complied, watching her every movement. She sank to her knees in front of him and kissed the inside of his knees. Her fingers tingled as they ran from his calves up the outsides of his thighs.

"My turn to taste you," she whispered.

The first touch of her tongue on his velvety skin elicited a strangled curse from Zach. His hips jerked and he sucked in a breath as she wrapped both hands around him.

"Jesus, you have some talent." He arched back and closed his eyes.

Elizabeth had written this exact scene several times in her book, but in person, this was so much better. Bringing Zach pleasure only increased her own excitement. She could become addicted to his taste.

◻◻

BETH CONTROLLED the pace and teased him mercilessly and he was going to let her have her way, even if it killed him. And then he realized, in the next several minutes, that it might actually be possible to die of bliss. Her soft mouth was wrapped around him while his hands were plunged in her hair, feeling the silky strands caress his fingers.

Beth worked her mouth up and down taking him in a way that made his heart stutter. He thought he might explode when she hummed to herself, sending shivers throughout his entire body.

"You have no idea how good that feels."

She hummed again and he started to lose control.

Enough was enough. Her playing was driving him out of his mind with the need to throw her on the bed and take her. Lifting her up, he turned the tables on her.

"My turn," he growled.

Using his shoulders to spread her long legs apart, he stared his fill at her glistening blonde curls. He licked her heat before stabbing his tongue into her wet channel. Her head thrashed back and forth, and he didn't think she was aware of her moans.

"Oh God, Zach," she moaned. "That feels incredible."

"You like that, baby?"

"I'm burning up."

"I want complete meltdown."

And that's what she gave him. Everything he asked for and more. He slid a finger inside and then two, and when he touched that special place inside of her, she catapulted over the edge. Only then did the sweet torment stop.

He kissed his way to her mouth. His tongue battled with hers, stealing her breath. He leaned over to the dresser drawer to get protection when she stopped him.

"I'm on the pill. Have been for years. I want to really feel you this time."

That was all he needed to hear. He entered her in one long thrust. He groaned as she sighed, feeling complete as he moved within her, fast and then slow. And when Beth reached up and palmed his face with her hands, he lost himself in her eyes. Her naked admiration humbled him and allowed him to rein in his control. He wanted to make this so good that she'd want to stay with him, even if it was just for this...this remarkable bond their bodies shared.

Her passion awed him. It was everything he'd ever fantasized about when he was alone at night...everything he could have ever dreamed of.

"You feel amazing."

Her hips lifted languidly to meet his slow thrusting, their bodies already in tune and working together to reach fulfillment.

Zach kissed her long and slow. "You are the amazing one."

He'd never been much of a breast man, but hers were perfect. They fit into his hands and mouth as if made for him. And she so was responsive to his touch. Every stroke of his tongue on her nipples had her clenching around him as he moved inside her.

Reaching down with one hand, he thumbed her most sensitive spot, drawing a low guttural moan from deep within her. He moved in and out of her, possessing her body, but wanting her soul. He couldn't hold back any longer, so he increased his pace, sending her into another orgasm.

"That's it. Come for me," he rasped. "Belong to me."

"Yeesss, Zach. Anything."

He convulsed inside her, tense muscles loosening in an all-consuming explosion. When he was spent, he leaned down to kiss the woman he loved. Her lips were lightly swollen from his passion and she had a glazed look in her eyes.

She looked satisfied. He wished he could be content with the passion only.

Whether she accepted it or not, she was his life. Everything he'd done was for her, to make a life for them both. He knew that now. He'd been on autopilot since leaving the Marines, but his world had always been her. Every step taken with the intent of having her share a life with him, he just hadn't realized it until she'd come to him for help.

Now he just had to convince *her* that they belonged together for more than just a moment of time.

CHAPTER 9

*S*aturday morning dawned bright and clear.

Zach had hiked over to Jesse's place for some tools, so Elizabeth decided to walk the mile out to the road to check the mail. She needed to clear away the cobwebs in her head, because book two in her series wasn't going to write itself.

She showed up just as the postman pulled up to the box.

"Good morning to you, miss," he said in a chipper voice. He was a nice-looking older man in a perfectly pressed blue uniform. Steel gray hair glinted in the bright morning sun. "You must be the Miss Russell that I have a package for."

"That would be me," she answered with a smile.

"I'm Henry, by the way. Pleased to meet you."

"I'm pleased to meet you too, Henry. Is everyone here this friendly?" she smiled. "This is my first visit to the area."

He laughed. "Actually no, that young man who lives here is a bit gruff and keeps to himself."

"Zach?"

"That'd be him. He usually glares at me when I bring his

mail. Unless it's a card from…now, let me see," he scratched his head. "What was that girl's name?"

"A girl?" She tried to sound uninterested, but knew she'd failed when he grinned.

"Oh yes, now I remember. It was a birthday card from you."

He chuckled, even took a moment to slap himself on the knee.

She huffed and put her hands on her hips. "I think you might have a mean streak."

"I saw that mad look come into your eyes, you can't fool old Henry. And, I say it's about time too, 'cause the only time that boy smiles is when I'm giving him a card from you."

He reminded her of Bea, always meddling. Usually with good intentions. And Henry was clearly interested in the love lives of others. She wondered if he read the mail too.

"I almost forgot your package," he said, ambling back to his mail truck.

He handed her the package and the rest of Zach's mail and stuck his hand out to shake.

"It was lovely to meet you. I hope to see you again."

"It was nice to meet you too. See you around." She smiled and waved as he drove away.

Elizabeth walked back in a haze. Henry's little joke and her instant jealousy made her realize something important. She'd had strong, but confused feelings for Zach since she was in high school and terrified that her father would find out somehow. But this was different. This was more—overwhelming.

Jesus, she was in love with him.

This was the grown up stuff. The kind of love that was messy, all-consuming, and irrational. The kind of love that made a person insane enough to consider something that terrified her.

It made her want to please him, and that was beyond scary. Because, what if she lost herself? Lost her hard-won independence? Became a ghost of the person she was now, because of love?

Just like her mother.

◻◻

"Never mind, she just walked in," Zach said, as Elizabeth walked through the front door. "Yeah, thanks."

She couldn't believe the anger on his face as he came striding towards her.

"Where have you been?"

The soft tone was more menacing than any shouting he could have done and it jerked her out of the haze she'd been in walking back. Then he reached out and wrapped his arms around her, roughly pulling her into his chest for a bear hug.

Elizabeth wrapped her arms around his middle, shaking her head at his worry. The mail slipped from her fingers as she returned his hug. He tugged at her hair, forcing her head back to meet his eyes.

"You're going to give me a heart attack."

"I just went to check the mail. I stayed on the property. Nothing happened."

"Yet. Nothing happened yet. You're not out of danger."

And then he kissed her. He scorched her with his touch, making her forget the danger. Zach was everything good in her life, her rock, her family, her lover. And he kissed her like she was the prize from some Viking raid.

Elizabeth was so lost in the kiss that it was a moment before she realized there was a noise intruding. She opened

71

her eyes and found that she was literally wrapped around Zach.

He stared at her a moment longer before putting her down.

"That's your phone," Zach said softly, when she looked confused. He dug the phone out of her back pocket and handed it to her. She took it with shaky hands.

"Hello?"

"Hey there, how's all that mountain air treating you?" Her landlord's cheerful voice was a cool splash of water to her overheated body.

"You're not getting out of talking about your lack of safety sense." Zach's look was serious and she knew she was in for another lecture.

She nodded and focused on the call. "Hey, Bea. How are you?"

"Wondering if that man is as sexy as his voice?"

Elizabeth grinned. Bea had a one-track mind and not a shy bone in her body. Zach raised an eyebrow when she looked at him, but he didn't ask any questions.

"Yes, he is."

"I could tell. Good ones are hard to find these days."

"So what's up?"

"I've got some bad news for you. Your apartment was broken into again."

"You've got to be kidding. What happened?"

Elizabeth bit her lip and looked up into Zach's concerned face. He took her hand and led them both to the couch to sit down.

"I'm putting you on speaker so my friend, Zach, can hear, okay?"

"Sure. It's the damnedest thing. Whoever broke in this time put everything back in place. I have to tell you, it makes the hair on my body stand up just thinking about it. Even the books are in the right order again. The weirdo even vacuumed."

"Did you call the police?"

"I sure did. That sexy detective came out to look it over. But that's not the worst of it," Bea's voice quivered just a bit. "He broke into my place as well. I must have been sleeping. I never heard a thing."

"I am so sorry. You weren't hurt, right?"

"Not so much as a scratch. I surely don't understand it and the police just looked confused. I have to say, doesn't give me much confidence in the system."

"Did he take anything or destroy anything?" Elizabeth asked.

"Didn't take anything that I could find except my address book. Gives me the willies knowing he was here while I was sleeping."

"So, it's possible that he only broke into your place to get this address?" Zach's calm question broke into the conversation.

Beth could feel the shock on her face. Oh God. It had been so stupid to leave the house. He could be here already and she'd been out in the open. She might as well have just screamed 'victim here.'

"That's what that nice Detective Wolfe thinks," Bea confirmed. "He told me not to worry you with this, that his team would handle it. But I say, forewarned is forearmed."

"Thank you so much for calling. Jesus, I wouldn't blame you if you evicted me."

"Bullshit. You didn't cause any of this. Some psychopath has decided that he has a beef with you and did some damage. So what. None of this is your fault."

"Still, this is exposing you and the other tenants. What if something happened to one of them, like Mr. McCreedy or old Mrs. Walters on the third floor?"

"I happen to know that Eileen Walters has a sawed off shotgun hidden in her room and McCreedy packed a bag and took off, saying he'd be back on Monday."

"Isn't that a bit odd?"

"What, McCreedy or Eileen's shotgun?"

"Mr. McCreedy, I mean, he never leaves his apartment."

Bea paused. "Well, I never thought about that, but you're right. This isn't like him. Not at all."

"What do you know about him, Bea? I mean, do you think he's capable of something like this?"

"I'm aiming to find out," she said grimly.

"Might I suggest you let Wolfe handle this, ladies?" Zach said.

He was right. Bea shouldn't be snooping around Mr. McCreedy's apartment. What if he found out and became violent? She shuddered at the thought of Bea getting hurt.

"You might have a point," Bea said. "I'll give him a call back right now. You take care of Elizabeth."

"I will, Ma'am."

Tears were welling up. Just when she was beginning to feel safe again. "I'm scared, Zach. What if he comes here?"

"If he makes it this far, I'll take care of him. No one is going to hurt you, but you need to be more aware of your safety."

"I'm sorry."

He kissed her on the forehead. "I need to call a friend and let him know about McCreedy."

Elizabeth nodded, not wanting him to know how cold she felt when he let go of her. She didn't want to be that weak clingy woman. She had to be strong. Remembering the mail scattered by the front door, she got up to clean the mess.

That's when she saw the package.

She remembered that Henry had handed it to her, but she'd been so lost in her own world that she had never looked at it on the walk back to the cabin. In fact, she'd completely forgotten about it until now.

"Hey Zach," she said, staring at the package in a new light. "Can you look at the mail?"

Today's postage was on it with her name and Zach's address. No return address or name. She was suddenly very leery of touching it again.

"What is it?" Zach asked coming up behind her.

"I'm expecting a couple things in the mail, but nothing that would fit into a small box," she said, pointing at the package wrapped in brown paper. "Detective Wolfe is sending some victim's affidavit, but that would have been in a flat envelope. And I'm sure it would have a return address."

"Bring me a Ziploc bag and the tongs from the kitchen drawer."

She ran into the kitchen and got the items he requested. She returned and watched as Zach examined the box.

"Fuck." He turned the package over with the tongs. "This was mailed from right here in Flagstaff."

"But it was mailed today, the post office isn't that fast."

He pointed to the label off to the side. "Express delivery. This is still a small community. Small enough to make sure this package made it here today."

He pulled a large pocket knife from his jeans and used the blade to slice open the tape. With the tongs he carefully opened the box and pulled out what was inside. It looked like some kind of silky material that was a dark forest-green color.

"Oh God. Those are mine."

Bile rose up and burned her throat. In the grip of the tongs was the pair of underwear that had been stolen from her dresser during the first burglary.

"Beth," Zach said. "Elizabeth," he said in a louder voice, snapping her out of her stupor.

"Uh huh, I'm okay," she managed. Her voice shook.

"I need the Ziploc, honey. I don't want to touch these, they might have evidence on them." His tone was grim. "Let me get them in the bag and then we can put them out of sight."

She handed over the bag, nodding. "I'm fine, really, it was just a shock."

"I know. You're doing great, and you are safe here."

His face was completely devoid of any emotion. He was in Marine mode and only his eyes gave away any indication of what he felt. It should have terrified her, that look in his eyes.

That look said that he could, and would, kill anyone that threatened her.

"I need to call the police," she said.

He nodded and kissed her on the forehead as he stood. "Make the call."

⬚⬚

HE WATCHED from his hiding spot as she stepped outside, rubbing her arms as if she were cold. Her long blonde hair was down, wavy around her shoulders. She scanned the trees and he held his breath when she seemed to look right at him.

You feel me here, don't you? Just like you could feel me in your apartment. Did you like the rose I left for you?

The moment was lost when a large man with dark hair came outside and joined Elizabeth on the wooden porch. She turned away and went into his open arms. And when she turned her face up for a kiss, he could feel the anger swell.

How dare she kiss another man.

And yet, watching her stirred his body. He wanted to be the one kissing her, holding her...controlling her. He'd put in the time and effort to show his devotion and he would make sure she was properly impressed.

But she would have to be purified first.

He waited until the man led Elizabeth back inside the cabin. Then he backed away carefully. It took him ten minutes to get back to his car and another hour to reach the little motel he'd rented for the week. It never hurt to be overly prepared.

He shook off his jacket as he entered the shabby room. It served his purposes and when Elizabeth was purified enough for him, he would take her somewhere nicer. Pulling the duffle bag out from under the bed, he took inventory.

Duct tape.

Nylon rope.

Tranquilizers.

Whip.

He nodded to himself as he looked at the rest of the supplies. He still needed a couple of things, but he had the essentials. His checked the 9mm Glock as well, making sure it was loaded and ready.

The big man was a complication. He'd have to make sure to neutralize him or get him out of the way before he made his move. Elizabeth was his and it was time she found that out.

She would learn.

They always did.

CHAPTER 10

*I*t had taken Beth some time before she was calm enough to make the call. She'd insisted on doing it herself. And yet, she looked like she was going to throw up or pass out. Maybe both.

And Zach was furious.

He wanted this bastard caught and caged as soon as possible. Dead was preferable, but he didn't want his girl to see him kill, if at all possible. He had too many marks against him as it was. He wanted to marry her and have a family, and Beth was scared. Scared of commitment and scared that Zach would somehow morph into some sickly controlling person that would keep her locked up.

"Detective Wolfe is coming to get the box."

Zach turned at the sound of her tired voice. She stood with her arms crossed, staring outside the back sliding door.

Moving towards her, he slid his arms around her and pulled her unresisting body back against his. She relaxed against him immediately. Her hair was soft against his face as he gave her his support.

"When did he say he would be here?"

"He said he was only an hour away. I guess he was headed here anyway to have me review and sign my statement. He decided not to mail it, after all; he said it was easier to just make the drive and get it filed. And I'm sure he's going to tell me about the most recent break-in to my apartment. He wouldn't want to do that over the phone."

Zach tightened his arms. "You are not leaving my sight until this is over."

"I'm safe here."

But he heard the tremble in her voice. "Don't lie to yourself, Beth. You're safe with me, not here alone. And since Jess and I have some business that can't be put off, I want you with me."

Her shoulders stiffened.

"Don't freeze up on me."

She pulled away from him and whirled. There was fire in her eyes and, while he was glad to see her spunky nature returning, now wasn't the time. She jabbed one of her slim little fingers into the center of his chest.

"I need space and air sometimes. I can't stay cooped up and I won't be dragged around."

"This sick son of a bitch knows where I live. It. Is. Not. Safe."

"I have my phone and this place is a fortress of security. You've made it safe."

He could feel his teeth clench over her stubbornness. The woman was going drive him to drink. "That hasn't stopped you from going outside and leaving the alarm disarmed. How is that going to protect you? And no house is impenetrable. The windows can be broken. The doors kicked in."

Her eyes were wide as she stared at him and Zach realized that he'd been yelling. He took a deep breath to calm down.

79

"Look. All I'm saying is that, until this asshole is under arrest, it would be safer if we stayed together."

She crossed her arms over her chest. "I know I'm being difficult. I know it's irrational, but--"

"But you can't stand being told what to do. Especially by a man. By me."

She shook her head. "But I know I need to go, that I need to listen. It's just hard. Can you try and understand?"

Zach loved her, but her capitulation made him suspicious. And damn it, he had a meeting with Jesse that he couldn't get out of. He didn't want that detective in his home. He'd call the man and give him the address to the shop in town. He could talk to Beth at the café across the street. He'd give her the space she thought she needed.

"I'll try if you will. Go get ready, we're leaving for town in ten minutes."

Beth nodded and, because he couldn't stop himself, he leaned forward and took her lips with his before she turned and went back into the bedroom. He needed her like he needed air and he'd be damned if her own stubbornness would get in the way of his protecting her.

He had a phone call to make. Beth might think he was compromising, but there was no way in hell he was leaving her alone with Detective Wolfe. And he had some friends that worked for his company from time to time who were almost as lethal as he and Jesse were.

Someone would be close to her the entire time. And neither one of them would ever know.

Zach made her crazy.

She was trying to cope. And sometimes being stubborn was the only thing that kept her from curling into a ball of pathetic weeping mush. She'd worked hard on her independence after her tyrannical father died, and she wasn't giving that up for Zach or anyone else.

Detective Wolfe was leaning against his white Crown Victoria when they arrived in town.

"He certainly made good time," Zach muttered.

"He's just doing his job."

"If he was doing his job, he would have caught this scumbag already."

Beth stopped herself from rolling her eyes. "Stop being snarly and go to your meeting. I'm going across the street to the café you suggested with Wolfe. I'll stay inside and have him escort me back when we're through."

She got out, holding the plastic bag containing the package and her undies. Zach was right behind her as she handed the bag over to Wolfe.

"Thanks for coming," she said.

Taking the bag from her, he slipped it into the trunk of his car and retrieved a brown folder full of papers. She assumed they were the ones she was to sign.

"Just making sure all the paperwork is in place for when we catch this guy," he replied.

Zach grunted quietly before turning Elizabeth in his arms. "Stay in the café with the cop. You're safer in a crowd. Do not go anywhere alone."

"What about the ladies room?" she sassed.

"Hold it until you get back to this office."

She smiled and tried to reassure her big man by giving him a quick peck on the lips. Zach stopped glaring at Wolfe long enough to give her a hug.

"Take care of her, Wolfe."

The Detective nodded, "I will."

Done with the macho posturing, Elizabeth shook her head, turned and strode across the street toward the little café that Zach said had the best croissants in Flagstaff. She didn't stop until she was at the counter ordering a chocolate-filled croissant and a hot chocolate. It was shaping up to be one of those days where chocolate plus more chocolate was the only fix.

Looking around, Elizabeth spied an empty spot and headed toward it. The man in the next booth looked up as she approached and nodded before going back to reading his paper. He was tall and lean, and when he'd looked at her, she got the weird feeling that he recognized her.

"So, I guess you have a boyfriend after all."

She shook her head at herself for imagining things and looked up at Detective Wolfe as he slid into the booth across from her. The big window allowed her to look across the street at Zach and Jesse's business. It made her feel better, being able to look at it and know he was just on the other side of the door. And she wasn't exactly sure what Zach was anymore, but boyfriend didn't seem the right word.

She noticed his plain coffee and glazed donut. "Guess the cop stereotype is accurate as well."

He chuckled. "Hey, everyone loves donuts, not just cops."

Elizabeth grinned back at him. "True enough."

"Tell me about Mr. Steele and his partner," he said, flipping open the brown folder and sliding a pen out.

She sighed. "I went to high school with Zach. I've known him a long time."

"And you trust him?"

"With my life, Detective."

"Okay, so why not mention him or his partner? Have you had problems with them?"

"No. I didn't mention Zach because he's not a part of any of this. He would never do anything to hurt me. Anything."

And she realized that she meant it. She'd always known that Zach was capable of violence and, when he went into the military, it had made her nervous. She'd put a wedge of distance between them because of that.

It had been a purely instinctual move.

She, who had always been fearful of large, controlling men, found herself in love with a warrior. One who was used to giving orders and being obeyed. And she wasn't the least bit scared by it. Not anymore. Zach's iron control was his strength and Elizabeth knew that power would never be turned against her. *That* was the difference in men like Zach and Jesse. They had tempers like normal people, but they had the self-control men like her father didn't possess. And Zach really was only a fanatic about her safety.

"Ms. Russell?"

"Sorry, Detective. Just stunned by this whole turn of events."

"We will catch this guy, I promise."

She forced a smile. "I know you will."

"What can you tell me about Jesse Calhoun?"

"Only that his mother named him after a famous bank robber, he has six sisters and was a Marine with Zach. Zach trusts him, so I trust him."

While he wrote in his notebook, Elizabeth drank her hot chocolate and tried to understand how being in love with Zach might change how she felt about commitment. What was stopping her?

She was beginning to face the fact that she had been a coward most of her life. Avoiding emotional entanglements was safe, but lonely. Being with Zach opened her eyes to the possibility of more.

She didn't want to live life behind protective glass anymore. This whole bizarre situation she was in made her realize that life wasn't safe. In a weird way, Elizabeth was grateful that she'd been shaken out her emotionless rut.

Otherwise, she might have lived her whole life never being brave enough to take a chance.

"Why don't I sign those papers so you can get back to Phoenix and your investigation?"

"Of course." He slid some papers toward her, along with his pen. "This is your statement and an inventory of everything found broken or listed stolen by you."

"Victim statement," she read aloud. "I hate that word. Victim. It makes me feel small and useless."

"It's just a word, Ms. Russell," he said kindly. "It doesn't have to be a mindset."

And she wouldn't let it be any longer. She'd lived too long as a victim and she'd been just waiting to be put in that role again. Expected it. That's why she was so stubborn and resistant. Amazing how one little word suddenly made so much sense. Explained so much about her. She shook her head to clear it.

"Tell me about the third break-in, Detective."

His expression said he wasn't surprised by her knowledge. "The landlady."

Elizabeth shrugged. "She cares about me."

"I can understand why." Then he looked away out the window. "I wanted to find a way to break it to you gently."

"That my burglar is sick and twisted? I figured that one out already." She stared at the half-eaten croissant, knowing she'd never finish it with the change in conversation. "What is the motivation for breaking in to clean up?"

"I don't know. It's almost like he's atoning for the first two. Making it up to you somehow."

"Okay, that freaks me out even more."

"I wish I could tell you something concrete. This is just a feeling."

They finished their drinks in awkward silence after that. She could tell he wanted to ask more questions about Zach, but decided against it. When he abruptly stood, she followed him outside and to his undercover cruiser.

As she watched Wolfe drive away, two things caught her attention. One was the man who sat in the booth next to her seemed to be watching her. The other was someone who shouldn't have been in Flagstaff, because he never left his apartment.

Mr. McCreedy.

Elizabeth backed up and off the sidewalk, pressing her back to the building. She was partially hidden in the shadow of the overhang and a sign that was advertising the real estate office next door.

What was he doing here?

McCreedy was dressed in dark clothing and kept looking over his shoulder as he walked. He was maybe two hundred yards away and across the street. She wouldn't have noticed him at all, if it hadn't been for that ratty leather jacket he always wore. It was bomber style and covered in patches from his travels. The one that caught her attention was a bright red patch with a black widow spider on it. She couldn't remember where it was supposed to be from, but it always creeped her out.

The chocolate croissant that tasted so good earlier felt like a brick in her stomach. A brick that might make its way back up. God, she hated the instant fear. It could be a coincidence that he was here in Flagstaff. Zach didn't believe in coincidences. Maybe she shouldn't either.

She lost sight of him while she remained frozen in the shadows. And when she was able to make her legs move again, he was gone. The man in the café was gone as well. It suddenly seemed like an hour had passed when, in reality, it had been maybe a minute.

Zach.

She needed Zach to make her world right. The man she

loved with her entire being. He was her soul mate and it had only taken her most of her life to realize it. She was going to tell him, but not just yet. Right now, she needed his arms around her and she needed to be out from under the sword that was hanging over her head.

Then she'd say yes. Yes to moving in and yes to marrying him.

After a long engagement and when she was sure she wouldn't hyperventilate at the thought of walking down the aisle and tying her life to his.

She wouldn't be a victim any longer.

CHAPTER 11

*Z*ach found her frozen outside, before she could let the panic take over completely.

"What's wrong?"

Elizabeth came out of her stupor and threw herself into his arms. The warmth of his body seeped into her and he picked her up and carried her inside.

"What's wrong, baby? Did Wolfe say something or do something to you?"

Jesse brought over a jacket and wrapped it around her shoulders when Zach set her on their leather couch in the office. "Can I get you something darlin'?"

She shook her head no, refusing to let go of Zach. "It was my neighbor, Mr. McCreedy. I saw him out on the street, just as the Detective was leaving."

She saw Jesse and Zach give each other a look.

"It's just a coincidence, right? I mean, how could he know I was here?"

"I'm going to go check it out," Zach said.

"No," Jesse said putting a hand on Zach's shoulder to keep him sitting next to Elizabeth. "I've got this. You stay and make sure she's protected. Tell me what he looks like and what he was wearing."

"There was also a guy in the café that seemed like he was watching me," she said. Zach and Jesse exchange a look and wondered what that meant.

"I'll check that out too," Jesse said.

Once he got the descriptions, he was gone. And when he came back, McCreedy had taken off. No one in the stores remembered seeing him. He wasn't staying in any of the hotels or bed and breakfasts in town either. Jesse stayed in town to do some more investigating while Zach took her back to the cabin.

It was late; she was tired and edgy and she knew Zach was pissed. A hot shower and bed was her plan.

Elizabeth was under the hot spray of the shower when Zach joined her. It startled her for a moment as the cold air hit and raised goose bumps.

"I'm sorry about all this, Zach."

His warm and naked chest touched her back as his arms wound around her body.

"It was stupid and reckless to just stand out on the street with no one around. I should've gone directly inside where it was safer."

He never said a word as he turned her in his arms and pressed his lips to hers. He consumed her then, with just his body touching hers and his lips devouring her mouth; she went up in flames.

Her silent warrior. Still mad and taking it out on her by making her burn with desire. If this was her punishment, then she would gladly take it.

"Talk to me," she whispered.

"No."

"Damn it, Zach."

His teeth teased her lips, nipping and biting until she

opened on a sigh. His tongue thrust in and tangled with hers. Using his body, he pressed her up against the wall, angling the shower head so that the hot water hit them both.

And then he went to work on her body. Plumping and plucking her nipples until they were hard and standing at attention, waiting for more. He wasn't gentle and she didn't want him to be. She wanted to be taken. Anything could happen and, if they only had these few days together, then she wanted all of him. Everything he could give.

"Oh God, that feels good," she moaned.

His warm mouth feasted on her breast while one hand moved lower, caressing her hips and cupping her bottom. He pulled her pelvis forward into his sex as he rubbed himself against her.

Her body shuddered at the contact.

She pulled his hair to try to force his mouth up to hers, but he was having none of it. Instead he dropped to his knees and moved one of her legs over his shoulder. The spray of the water hit her chest and forced her eyes closed, just as she felt his tongue.

His tongue went to work and her knees buckled. Strong hands held her pressed against the shower wall as Zach plundered her with his mouth. Sucking and kissing and pulling noises out of her that didn't even sound human.

When she cried out and convulsed, he lapped up every drop of her orgasm.

And he still never said a word. He dipped his tongue into her bellybutton before paying homage to her nipples once more. He took her lips and swallowed her sigh.

Nothing was as sweet as his tongue with her flavor.

Gripping her legs in each hand, Zach lifted her body and wrapped her legs around his waist. The tip of his shaft was poised at her entrance. Slowly, so slowly, he brought her down until she was impaled. Stretched and full, the throbbing started over again.

"Zach," she whispered, tonguing the shell of his ear. That's all she could say, just his name.

And when he moved, he pulled almost all the way out of her and surged back in. Her back slapped the tile as pleasure streaked up from her core. Zach moved like a machine, thrusting in and out of her in steady strokes designed to drive her out of mind. She couldn't move, pinned as she was between his big wet body and the wall.

All she could do was take everything he was. Accept who he was.

Elizabeth held on as he pounded into her. Her thighs quivered as she held on. She raked her nails up his back and bit the side of his neck before kissing the same spot.

"You make me burn," she whispered into his ear.

Zach pulled back and looked deeply into her eyes, his face taut with desire. Keeping her lower body pinned with his, he laced his palms with hers and held her hands above her head.

And then he went completely wild.

ZACH HAD PLANNED on making love to Beth until all her fear was gone. Maybe silence and his body would finally get through to her stubborn brain. Talking wasn't doing anything for him. But he got lost in her body like he always did.

He gave himself over to her, body and soul, showing her his love with every stroke, every thrust. He wouldn't speak, so he took her luscious mouth and tasted her sweetness.

Her sex gripped him like a hot glove as he surged in and out of her and when he felt her inner walls contracting around him, he stroked her harder.

And she melted around him.

His Beth came apart so beautifully in his arms that he could have happily died right at that moment. He let her arms fall around his neck as he moved her body lower on the wall, thrusting into her as deeply as he could. Once, twice and finally a third thrust and he erupted in his own orgasm, spurting into her over and over.

The force of his climax triggered another one for his woman and she tensed up and milked him, squeezing him as she came a third time.

He loved it. Loved her. And her independent spirit. A spirit he could only protect, not crush just because it would keep her safe.

Damn.

Letting her slide down his body, Zach washed her thoroughly as well as himself. Beth let him dry her and tuck them both into bed before she said anything.

"I'm sorry, Zach."

He sighed. "I know, baby. I'm sorry too."

She sat up, dragging the sheet with her and stared at him with her large chocolate-brown eyes. "What are you sorry about? I'm the moron who doesn't listen."

Reaching up, he brushed her hair to the side and tucked the rogue strands behind her ear. She was everything that was beautiful in his world. His light, his smile, his heart. If anything happened to her, he would die. But he couldn't keep her in a cage or behind glass, because then she would die. Or leave him.

And that, he couldn't stand.

"I just realized that I can't squelch any part of your nature. I shouldn't demand that you stay shut away. I know how much you need your freedom, how much it scares you to be trapped in a situation you can't control."

Tears threatened to waterlog them both as she looked at

him. She blinked to keep them from falling. Then she smiled and leaned over to kiss him.

"No one has ever understood me the way you do."

"You just have to remind me now and then that I'm being a controlling asshole."

She laughed and stretched out beside him, curling her warm naked body into his side. Stroking her fingers up and down his chest, she was quiet for a while. Those light touches were driving him crazy, and, coupled with the feel of her soft breasts rising and falling with her breathing, his sated body roared back to life.

"How about we compromise?" she finally said, breaking the silence.

"Hmmm," he murmured, already distracted.

"You stay with me and I will follow your rules. No leaving the property or going anywhere without you. And I won't even complain about your overbearing protectiveness."

Zach didn't have to think at all about it. The meeting in town earlier was the last one for a while and he'd already told Jesse that he would be holed up in the cabin until Beth was safe.

"Deal."

And when her hand moved lower under the blanket, he stopped thinking at all.

CHAPTER 12

*E*lizabeth forced herself to relax. Small half-moon grooves covered her palms due to her nails digging in. Through the window of Zach's truck, she could see him standing with three of the local police officers and Detective Wolfe. They were talking outside of the manager's office at a little bed and breakfast place in Sedona.

Mr. McCreedy was in one of those rooms.

A little less than an hour outside of Flagstaff, Sedona was host to millions of tourists per year. It was a great place to blend in, but Jesse Calhoun was part bloodhound. No one hid from him for very long.

And since Zach had agreed to her deal, Elizabeth had demanded to come along for the ride. Jesse was outside the window of the truck, standing guard. No one was coming near her without having to go through him.

Rolling down the window, she asked, "What's happening?"

Jesse shrugged. "Since I can't hear anything, my guess is they're trying to decide how to play this. They didn't have time for a warrant, so the bastard is going to have to invite them into his room so they can look around."

"So what happens if he won't let them in?"

"Then Zach and I stake out his place until he leaves. Then, we break in and nose around."

Elizabeth could feel her eyebrows rise up into her hairline. "But that's illegal."

Jesse looked her in the eye. "If this is the sick son of a bitch that broke into your apartment three times and continues to terrorize you, then we're going to make him pay. One way or another."

She shivered at the finality in his tone. Zach had said basically the same thing, but hearing it from Jesse made it seem more real, for some reason. Maybe it was because she didn't know him as well. When Zach told her he would protect her by any means, it made sense, but why would Jesse?

"Why are you doing this? I don't want you to get hurt."

His blue eyes blazed down into hers with an intensity that would have normally scared her right into her grave. But it didn't. His intensity made her feel safe. It was an odd feeling and one she had only ever gotten around Zach.

"Why?" he asked.

She nodded.

"Because he loves you, that's why." He nodded toward Zach, who stood with his arms folded across his chest as he listened to Detective Wolfe.

"You make him smile and I've never seen him smile like he does when he looks at you."

"I love him, too." She whispered it, afraid that saying it out loud might somehow make it less real. Might somehow destroy the trust she was beginning to put into the feeling.

"You'd better."

That harshly spoken statement forced a small smile out of her. "You love him too, don't you?"

"Like the brother I never had. We've been through Hell together and he's always got my back, no questions asked. And I've got his."

Elizabeth reached out and touched his arm. "Thank you for that. For taking care of him, and being his friend. He doesn't make friends easily. Or trust people." She shrugged ruefully. "It's a product of the foster system."

"I've got your back too, Beth."

Emotion clogged her throat that this big man, a deadly warrior in his own stead, was offering to be her friend too. He'd shown her nothing but kindness and now he was standing guard over her. Protecting her back while Zach tried to figure this out.

"I've got yours too, Jesse."

He winked and bowed slightly at the waist. "I'm honored, Ma'am."

He was making fun, but she didn't mind. That was his way. Elizabeth had noticed that when she asked him anything personal, his accent would suddenly thicken. Jesse didn't like to talk about himself or his past.

She could understand that. Everyone had scars and that was the way he chose to hide his. For herself, it had been isolation. From people, from memories, from life.

And she was sick of it.

ZACH DIDN'T LIKE BEING TOLD no. The Sedona police sergeant in charge of this "knock and talk" seemed competent enough, and he made it clear that he wasn't about to let a civilian through that door first.

Glancing back towards his truck, he saw Beth and Jesse talking. No one suspicious hanging around, and yet, he couldn't shake the feeling that unfriendly eyes were on him. Worse, those eyes were on Beth.

Detective Wolfe was putting some serious mileage on his police-issued cruiser, going back and forth from Flagstaff to Phoenix. Zach didn't like the man. He'd seen the way the detective looked at Beth and, while he couldn't blame him for wanting her, he'd break his damned neck if he stepped out of line.

The loud *bang-bang-bang* on the door pulled Zach's attention.

"Darwin McCreedy. This is the Sedona Police Department and we'd like a word with you."

The door cracked open after a minute or so and a voice answered. "What is the meaning of this?"

"We have some questions for you, sir. Can we come inside?"

"I haven't broken any laws. What's this about?"

Zach couldn't see the man, his view being blocked by three of the officers, but the sound of the voice and inflection didn't sound right. He had experience in dealing with criminals in the military. Their voices held an edge, a menace that just wasn't present here. His shoulders relaxed and he stepped back. This wasn't the guy. Oh, Mr. Darwin McCreedy was hiding something, but he wasn't the one who was terrorizing Beth.

Zach would bet his life on it.

Shooting Jesse a look, he gave a quick shake of his head. Before Jesse could relax, he sent couple of quick hand signals that only his unit used. An unfriendly still had eyes on them and they still needed to be vigilant. He saw his friend take a casual look around. Zach did the same, but whoever watched them was hiding very well. Or hiding in plain sight.

The officers and Wolfe finally convinced the older man to let them inside. Zach automatically moved with them as they entered. It was spacious and the bay window on the opposite side of the door flooded the place with light.

The place was covered in different colored threads and patterns of some kind. The man himself was a bit of a surprise and, clearly, a cross dresser. His hair was slicked back and he wore men's jeans, but a flowered sweater. His blue eye shadow matched the color of the sweater.

"May we ask what you're doing in Flagstaff, sir?" Wolfe kept a straight face.

"Why is it anyone's business what I do?" His hands were on his hips as he looked around.

"Because you live in the same building as Elizabeth Russell and there is an ongoing investigation into the break-ins at her unit," Wolfe explained.

"Well, I don't have anything to do with that. Barely even know the girl."

"We understand that, but still, it is an odd coincidence that you showed up in the very place she is...during an investigation."

McCreedy shrugged and looked confused. Convincingly confused, to Zach's trained eye. "I saw the girl leave the other day, sure. Never asked her where she was going because it's none of my business. Just like my trip here is none of your business. A man needs a bit of privacy now and again."

"But why here specifically, sir?"

The older man sighed and took a step over to the table with a small mound of patterns. He picked one up and also took a business card from a neat stack at the center. "I do cross-stitch. Every year I come up to Flagstaff for the art festival."

Several of the local cops nodded, evidently knowing about the art fest.

"I sell my stuff from home. That's how I make up the difference in the pittance the government gives me and my retirement. But every year, I come to the festival and see old friends and grab new patterns."

And dress like he wanted without the neighbors knowing, Zach thought.

"I see," the Sergeant said. "You understand we were just checking it out. For the safety of the woman."

McCreedy nodded. "Terrible business. She's a lovely girl. I've been trying to find a wig in the color of her hair. Have you seen her hair? It's simply gorgeous."

Zach had heard enough. McCreedy wasn't the guy. He was a harmless art buff who liked to dress in women's clothing and do cross-stitch. Zach sighed. It would have been easier if it had been him.

He backed out of the room, catching the Detective's eye when he did. Wolfe followed him outside.

"He isn't involved," Zach said.

Wolfe shook his head. "No. This guy's harmless."

"You have any other leads yet?"

"Still waiting on DNA to come back." He shoved his hand into his hair. "I'll stay and finish up here. Tell Elizabeth that we will catch this guy."

Zach nodded and turned to cross the street. The feeling of being watched was gone. Whoever it was had lost interest for the moment. He didn't like not knowing who the enemy was or where they were coming from.

It made him edgy.

Beth's lips were pinched and her shoulders tensed when he reached the truck. He shook his head, "It's not him."

"How can you be sure?" she asked.

"Because he's here for a cross-stitch festival and looks very comfortable in women's clothes."

"Wow," Jesse said.

"Yeah, he makes an ugly woman."

Beth huffed out a quick breath and he could see her

slowly relax. He hated that this was keeping her stressed out. Zach wanted her happy and focused on him. And moving in with him. That was step one. Marriage and kids were a battle he'd fight later on. He'd be happy if she'd finally agree to just live with him.

Permanently.

CHAPTER 13

"It's a diversion," Zach said. His tone was low and angry.

Elizabeth looked up from her computer. They'd been home for several hours and she'd been writing while Zach worked at the table on his laptop. She had been jarred out of her story when Zach's cell rang.

"Of course I'm not leaving, but you'd better get over there and see what the damage is. Yeah, got it. Call me."

"What happened?"

He looked like he was controlling the impulse to crush his phone. Dark brows formed an angry line and the tic in his jaw had started. "Someone started a fire in the back of our business."

"Oh my God." Jerking to her feet, Elizabeth went and put her arms around him and pressed her face into his chest. "This is because of me."

"Jesse is heading over now to see what can be salvaged."

"I'm so sorry. If it wasn't for me, none of this would be happening."

Ramming the phone into his back pocket, Zach shook his

head. "None of this is your fault, Beth. Not one bit of it, do you hear me?"

Looking into his stormy eyes, she could only nod. She hoped to appease him because it was her fault. If they lost the building, it would be because of her and her rotten luck in attracting the attention of a psychopath.

Elizabeth sometimes wondered if her life was cursed. The only thing convincing her that it wasn't was standing in front of her.

"Okay," she let out a strained laugh. "None of this is my fault. But you should go with Jesse."

Even before he shook his head, she knew he wasn't about to leave.

Then his phone chirped. Yanking it out of his pocket, he answered, "What now?"

Elizabeth followed when he went and pulled open the front door. The black plume of smoke outside couldn't have been from town. That was too far away. This looked like it was coming from the road.

"Goddammit! I'll be right there with some extinguishers."

"What's on fire?" she asked.

"The mailboxes out front and several of the big pines. Jesse needs me out there. If we don't get those out, and fast, it could turn into a forest fire."

"You need to go. We're surrounded by woods here and I don't want your home to burn. Or Jesse's."

She watched his face while he struggled with the need to stay and protect her and his need to get that fire out.

"Go. I'll be fine. You showed me how to use the gun in the table by the door. I can protect myself with that. I promise."

Obviously making his decision, he pulled her close and kissed the breath right out of her.

"Stay inside and stay safe."

"I will."

He ran through the house and gathered up the three fire extinguishers inside while calling the fire department to tell them of the fire and the address. Elizabeth stayed out of the way and, when he turned at the door to look at her, she got up on her tip-toes and gave him another quick kiss.

"Go."

She stepped outside, put her hands in her jeans pockets and turned her face up into the brightness of the sun. Zach was at a dead run toward the column of smoke. She watched until he was out of sight and then she turned to go back into the house.

Zach was right. She was safer inside under lock and key while he did his best to contain that fire. A faint rustling from the bushes pulled her head around to the far side of the porch. She squinted and saw a figure emerging from the foliage.

"Well, well. Lover boy finally left you alone for a moment. How fortuitous."

"DAMN IT, Mike! What do you mean you lost him?" Zach roared into the phone.

He started pacing, listening to his end of the conversation. "All you had to do was babysit for a couple hours."

Jesse stood still, listening to Zach's side of the conversation. His face was covered in ash and grime. Zach was sure his face matched. The mailboxes were out, but they couldn't reach the fire creeping up the tall pines and hitting the canopy. The lack of wind was helping, but if the fire department didn't get there soon, it was going to spread.

And now this shit. It was game time and they were already behind.

"Pray, Mike. Pray that nothing happens."

Zach hung up and faced his best friend. "It seems Detective Wolfe has had a little evasive-maneuver training. Mike lost him in traffic."

"Shit." Jesse tensed and then went calm. "Call it, Zach. Where do you need me?"

Jesse's Jeep was parked nearby, since he had been planning on going into town to check on the business. Zach never gave the business any more thought and neither did Jesse. This was about protecting one of their own—Beth.

"I need you to check the perimeter. You're the best tracker and I need to know if someone has been on my land. Go in quiet and ready. The bastard might already be here."

"Got it."

"Jess," Zach started, "Mike said his contact got ahold of him. DNA finally came back and confirmed our suspicions. He was able to pay off the right people, but Mike found an old report that confirms his involvement with a previous murder case. So watch your ass."

"Always do," Jesse said. "Go to your lady, I've got a bad feeling about this."

Then he melted into the bushes, making his way toward the cabin. Silent and deadly, Jesse would meet up with him back at the house.

Zach turned to go back to the cabin and felt the hair on his neck stand up. His instincts had saved his life more than once. Shit, he *was* already here. Zach could feel it. He took off at a dead run, dialing Jesse's cell.

"He's already here," he said when Jesse picked up. He didn't have to say anything more as he concentrated on getting to the cabin as fast as he could, knowing Jesse would have his back. He did what he'd told Mike to do.

He prayed.

"What are you doing here, Jeffery?"

Elizabeth was stunned to see him walking around the porch. His eyes darted back and forth before settling on her. He was dressed for hiking and his coat and pants had snags and leafy debris on them. It was the look of someone who'd been out in the woods for a while. Even his normally neat hair was in disarray.

"I needed to check on the progress of the book. For the editors," he murmured. "You understand, right?"

"You could have called to get that. You didn't have to come all the way out here."

Chills raced down her spine when his eyes finally made contact with hers. The Jeffery she knew wasn't there. Only madness and cruelty looked back at her.

"You haven't been taking my calls, now have you? You ran off to play whore." He spit out the words venomously. "So I decided to pay you a visit, since you're my favorite client."

She flinched at the word and tone, but tried to keep him talking. "How did you find me?"

"You gave me your address, remember?"

"I never gave you this address, Jeffery."

"Hmmm, must have been your nice landlady." He shook his head as if to clear it. "You always call after I've left the office. I wonder if you do that on purpose?" he questioned, almost to himself.

Oh God, please let Zach come back soon.

Elizabeth edged backward toward the front door. There was something wrong with Jeffery. Seriously wrong. Why hadn't she seen it before? She had to get to the gun.

"Elizabeth, my dear, you need to stop moving toward the door," he said, all pretense gone from his voice as he calmly pulled a small black revolver from the pocket of his coat and pointed it straight at her.

"W-what are you doing?" Elizabeth stammered. "I don't understand."

"It's very clear, darling. You ran away before I could fully express my affection for you. And don't worry, I'll forgive you for your little—indiscretion. Of course, I'll have to kill him. You need to understand that we are meant to be together. You and me."

"You broke into my apartment, didn't you?"

Even seeing the madness in his eyes, she needed to hear it from him…hear that he was the one making her life hell.

"I wanted you to know that you had my full attention. I hoped you would realize how much you mean to me." His tone was even, but his eyes were flat and cold. He still had the gun pointed at her as he narrowed his eyes.

"Why did you get the police involved?" He asked the question, but didn't seem to need a response from her. "I *told* you I would help you with someplace to stay. I could've taken care of everything for you."

Jeffery was gone and something else was in his place. Elizabeth didn't know when it had happened but he was 'out there;' he didn't realize how bizarre his actions were. He kept talking about how she was the perfect woman for him and that he knew it the first time they met. Calling him crazy would only make matters worse, so she kept her mouth shut.

"I should have listened to you, Jeffery."

Fear coiled through her stomach. She had to keep him talking.

They both heard the crunch of gravel from the front of the house. Someone was driving up. Jeffery gave a start and swiveled his head and the gun in that direction, giving Elizabeth the moment she'd been waiting for.

She took off in a full sprint toward the sound of the car, hoping that it was Zach and Jesse.

"Stop running, bitch."

Elizabeth put her head down and kept going. She ran in a

zigzag, hoping that Jeffery wasn't a marksman with his handgun.

Detective Wolfe jerked to a stop and was getting out of his Crown Victoria as she raced toward him.

"Gun! He's got a gun," she yelled.

He immediately pulled his own weapon and dropped into a crouch. "Get down."

Elizabeth had almost reached him when he started shouting and the shots rang out. Searing pain tore through her upper right arm, throwing her off-balance and sending her face-first into the gravel. The next shot went whizzing over where her head would have been and slammed into Detective Wolfe's chest.

He stumbled back and got one shot off that went high and wide. Her vision blurred, but she thought she heard Zach's voice. She wanted to see his handsome face so badly that she might have imagined hearing his voice.

"Zach," she whispered.

Sound muffled as the ringing in her ears increased and her stomach rolled and pitched. The pain in her arm overwhelmed her and the coppery smell of blood mixed with gun powder stung her nose. Her last thought before surrendering to unconsciousness was that she hoped she didn't throw up on Zach when she finally told him that she loved him.

"No!"

Zach launched himself, hitting the man hard in the back, using his superior size and the element of surprise to force the smaller man to the ground. The man rolled and hit Zach in the jaw, trying to knock him off and bring his gun up to fire.

"I'll kill you. You defiled her," he screamed.

Madness gave him strength as Zach wrestled with him in

the gravel. He squirmed, hitting out and kicking his legs. Zach punched him with one hand while keeping the hand with the gun pointed harmlessly out into the forest.

Jesse was there in an instant, having moved from his position in the thick brush. Jesse kicked the gun from Jeffrey's hand so hard that Zach thought he heard the bone crack. Jeffery's agonized scream and the odd angle of his wrist confirmed the break.

He thrashed and bucked. Zach punched him hard in the center of his chest, causing the air to whoosh out of his body. Then, he leaned forward with a forearm against Jeffrey's throat, cutting off any remaining air.

It only took a couple of moments before Jeffrey stopped struggling, his eyes rolled back and he went unconscious. Zach was up and running to Beth as soon as he felt the body under him go limp.

"Shoot him if he so much as twitches," he yelled back at Jesse.

"He's not going anywhere," Jesse responded.

"Beth," he whispered.

Zach landed on his knees next to her and pulled her into his arms. She was so white she was almost translucent and had scratches on her cheek and forehead from the fall. She still hadn't come around, so Zach used that moment to do a body check for breaks.

Finding none, he gently moved her arm towards him so he could check the gunshot wound she'd sustained. He ripped her sweater and saw the bullet had gone clean through the fleshy part of her upper arm, missing bone and major arteries.

Sighing with relief, he hugged her fiercely saying, "Come on, baby, wake up."

"Thanks for the caring, Steele," came a hoarse voice.

"You shouldn't even be here, Wolfe," Jesse said, coming

into the conversation. He dropped down next to where the Detective was leaning against his car to check the status of his wounds.

"You should have picked him up as soon as DNA came through," Zach snarled. "Instead, you left him loose and he was able to get here."

"You were wearing your vest. Good. That's the first smart thing you've done so far," Jesse broke in while he peeled the detective's shirt off. "You got lucky."

"We have procedures and protocols, Steele. Besides, the crafty bastard had already skipped town when the damn results came in. I figured he was here somewhere, since he obviously had the address," Wolfe snapped, ignoring Jesse. "How's Elizabeth doing?"

"She's been shot, that's how she's doing."

"Why'd you have someone tailing me?"

"I heard you were a hot-shot in the department and I wanted to make sure you had back-up in case you were tempted to try and arrest that maniac by yourself. Plus I didn't like that you had a prior connection with Beth."

"I'm touched, Steele. And I didn't even know about that until I started looking into her past."

"Don't be. I just didn't want you to fuck this up."

"If anyone cares, I called for the local cops and an ambulance," Jesse announced.

A soft moan stopped the arguing. All three men looked at Elizabeth. She opened her eyes and grimaced in pain. He couldn't help himself, he smiled. She was going to be okay.

"Why are you smiling?" she groused.

"Because you're not dead."

She blinked, confused. "Why does my arm hurt?"

"You were shot. How do you feel?"

Tears welled up in her eyes as she looked around. When she saw her agent, her breath caught and the tears rolled down her cheeks. Jesse had him tied up and he was still unconscious.

"I just can't believe it."

"It's over now. He'll never bother you again."

And when she started crying in earnest, he pulled her close and just held her.

CHAPTER 14

*E*lizabeth woke up groggy, trying not to move her right arm. As comfortable as Zach's bed was, it didn't cushion the pain. Maneuvering into a sitting position caused her to break a sweat.

"Ow, ow, ow."

It had been two days since the shooting, but her arm still hurt like crazy. She and Wolfe had been whisked away to the hospital where she'd had to stay overnight. Detective Wolfe had been released almost immediately after a cursory exam. His vest had taken the impact, like it was supposed to.

He'd stayed around, much to Zach's dismay, making sure she was doing well and to take the statements of everyone involved. He was adding to his case, but Zach groused that he was just hanging around to annoy everyone.

"What are you doing?" Zach came in with a tray of food.

"Trying to get comfortable," she complained.

"You're supposed to call me to help, damn it."

"I wanted to sit up by myself, damn it."

His lips twitched at her disgruntled tone and she couldn't help but smile back. He was such a growly bear and she loved him. Loved everything about him. From his protectiveness to his certainty that they belonged together. Too bad it took a psycho stalker and getting shot to make it sink in.

"What's going on with Jeffery?"

Zach set the tray down across her lap, fussed with some pillows and then sat next to her on the bed. Fluffy eggs, turkey bacon, potatoes and orange juice. The man knew how to make a good breakfast.

"Flagstaff police didn't take kindly to Jeffery showing up in their town and causing problems, so they filed their own charges for felony assault, attempted murder, as well as any other charge they could think of for shooting a fellow officer."

"And then he gets shipped back to Phoenix to face the charges pending there?"

He nodded. "He's going away for a very long time."

Elizabeth hoped that the feeling of helplessness that had taken over her life would eventually fade. She couldn't get that look out of her mind, the way his eyes changed and his voice changed. The insanity.

"I just don't understand why he went after me."

"My buddy, Little Mike, was looking into the investigation. Jeffery wasn't originally a suspect because he had an alibi. Turns out the alibi didn't hold, so he started digging into Jeffery's past. Your agent has been in and out of several very exclusive hospitals that specialize in treating mental disorders since he was a teenager."

"That was not on his resume when I was looking for an agent."

"He became fixated on a woman ten years ago and she ended up dead."

"Oh my God. That's horrible."

Zach shrugged. "There wasn't enough evidence of Jeffery's involvement to have him arrested and charged, just some witnesses that had seen him with the victim a couple of times. His family stepped in, hired a very good lawyer, and kept his name from being formally linked with the investigation."

"That was going to be me next, wasn't it?" She shivered again, thinking how close she had come to being his next victim.

Deciding not to dwell on it, Elizabeth turned her attention to Zach. He was shirtless and wearing a pair of baggy gray sweatpants. Her stomach growled, pulling a smile out of Zach as he held a fork up to her lips.

"I don't want my effort wasted this morning."

"I'm starved," she replied with a smile, looking him up and down while obediently opening her mouth.

"Mmm." She chewed and swallowed. "You're too good to me."

He stretched toward her and gave her a quick kiss. "You deserve it."

Then he pulled back, reached over and stole one half of her bagel.

"Where's your food?" She tried glaring at him because swatting at his hand wasn't working. She was actually full, but swatting at him while he stole bits of her breakfast had become a game they were playing.

"I already ate, but I'm hungry again." He looked at her breasts as he said it.

"You're always hungry," she laughed.

"Take the pills, Beth."

She stuck her tongue out at him before taking the antibiotic and pain killer that he had thoughtfully put on her tray. "Yes, sir."

"Sassy."

He got off the bed, making sure not to jostle her in any

way. Then he took the tray and disappeared down the hall and into the kitchen.

"Bully," she yelled down the hall.

While he was gone, she tried to think of the best way to broach the subject of their future. She'd been in too much pain to bring it up before, and then trying to sleep off the pain killers they had pumped her full of in the hospital.

Today was the first time she felt clear enough to actually talk to Zach. She bit her lower lip, thinking of the best way to tell him that she loved him. It's not like she could just blurt it out.

"What's going on in your head, Beth?"

She looked up, slightly startled, having never heard him re-enter the room. "What are you talking about?"

He leaned against the doorjamb, arms crossed over his muscled chest looking at her. Zach knew she'd been worrying. He always knew.

"What's in that locked room?"

He cocked his head to the side and raised an eyebrow, "Been driving you crazy, hasn't it?"

God, he was sexy. "You know it has!"

"Grouchy."

"Being shot has that effect on me."

He moved from the doorjamb and walked to her side of the bed. He threw the covers off of her and slid his arms under her knees and her back, easily lifting her from the mattress.

"Maybe you're finally ready. I hope to God that you are."

She thought she was going to have to argue with him and was at a loss when he gave in. There was a pinch of pain as he lifted her, but Zach was very careful about carrying her so that her arm moved very little.

Elizabeth took a deep breath and settled into his body,

113

loving his unique smell. Everything about him made her feel safe and loved. And she wanted all of it. All of him.

They stopped in front of the double doors that had been a massive curiosity for her. Okay, mild obsession. She wanted to see inside so badly that she was about to bounce herself out of his arms in excitement.

"Close your eyes and do not open them until I tell you," Zach commanded.

"Okay."

She was a little concerned about his tone. He actually sounded worried. She obediently closed her eyes but couldn't help teasing, "You don't have an entire room devoted to porn do you?"

Elizabeth smiled when she heard the heavy sigh and could just imagine the eye rolling he was doing. Well, she didn't *really* think he had a room full of porn, but it never hurt to ask.

She tightened her hold on Zach as she felt him dip down to open the door. He never struggled and she realized that the door must have been unlocked. She wondered if he had been planning on showing her the room anyway, before she asked.

"You already unlocked the door, didn't you?"

She felt his shrug. "You weren't in any condition to go snooping."

They moved through the doors and she could tell it was still dark inside. Zach set her down and told her not to move. The rustling sounded like the drapes covering the bay window. When the light hit her face, she knew she was right.

"Open your eyes, Beth."

She slowly opened her eyes, blinded by the light streaming in the windows. What she saw when her vision cleared, stunned her. She looked in every direction and suddenly she understood what Zach had accomplished in building this room.

He was telling her that he loved her, without ever saying the words. She knew it in her heart and soul, and, as she looked around in wonder, she knew he had built this room specifically for her.

Before all the trouble had begun.

"I can't believe you did this," she choked out.

It was the room she'd dreamed of growing up. She'd described it to Zach over and over again when they had their stolen moments at school. She never thought about an entire house, just one room that she could call her own.

A library.

She'd smuggled in so many books when her father had been alive. They were her escape when she was locked inside her room. Books gave her a window and life outside of her controlled existence. She loved the smell of the leather bindings, the feel of the pages on her fingers. Her own personal escape.

It was why she became a writer. To give someone else an escape from a life that might not be everything they'd hoped.

Tears began to fall as she looked at the floor-to-ceiling book shelves that were intricately designed and built into the walls. The bay window had three large panels of glass that faced the south part of Zach's property, so all that could be seen was sunlight and pine forest. The heavy drapes on either side were a deep royal blue with gold threads shot through that picked up the light. Directly underneath those beautiful windows was a built-in bench seat covered in a dark blue velvet material with pillows to match.

It looked like the perfect place to just sit and think, work out a plot problem, or simply read a book.

She turned and took in the rest of the room. Mounted to the front of the book cases was a fine brass railing with a delicate-looking ladder attached. She had always wanted a library with a rolling ladder so that she could climb to the top shelves.

There was only one book in the entire library and it was the one she had just written. Overwhelmed, she turned back toward the door to see Zach watching her with naked desire and something more.

"How did you remember?" she asked.

"I remember everything you've ever said to me."

He looked deep into her eyes, maybe searching for the same thing she was searching for. Zach was always so self-assured that it never occurred to her that he might be scared to tell her his feelings. She was never quite as sure of him as he seemed to be of her.

"Why did you build this room?" she asked softly, already knowing the answer, but needing him to say it.

"For you," he replied. "You've been the center of all my plans from the time we met."

"It was high school. How could you possibly know?"

"That I love you?"

She nodded.

"The moment I looked into those sad chocolate-brown eyes I knew. I was yours and you were mine. Mine to protect, and mine to love and cherish for the rest of our lives."

"Why didn't you ever tell me?"

"You needed time, baby. Time to grow up and find out who you wanted to be. And I needed to be able to provide for you, us, so I joined the Marines. Besides, you wouldn't have really believed me back then. I did propose. It was the best I could do back then."

He said it simply, with a shrug. All the hardships and sacrifices he'd made for her and he just shrugged it off as if it were the only option.

"I can't believe that I didn't see it. I've been such a coward.

Always running away from emotions and complications. Scared that I would somehow end up like my mother. Trapped. A shell of the person I could be."

She closed the distance between them and reached up to touch his cheek with her good arm.

"You're the most important person in the world to me, and I never looked close enough to realize it," she said.

"Do you know what the trouble with all my plans is?" he asked, nuzzling into her palm.

"No," she replied with a sniff.

"It doesn't work unless you love me. Even if you can't marry me. Just stay with me and let me love you...prove to you that we belong together."

It was hard to believe that she had fought against this for so long. Fought to stay away from the one person who loved her, despite her screwed up childhood. She'd always known that she loved him, but she'd refused to acknowledge that she was in love with him.

"I love you with all my heart, Zach. I have for forever, but I was never brave enough to tell you. And I promise you, I will love you for the rest of my life."

He hugged her to him fiercely, making sure that he didn't jostle her injury. Even then, he protected her. That was only one of the traits she loved about him; there were so many.

Zach would never be a talker, and he wasn't the type of man to tell her that he loved her often, but she would know. He would show her in every way he knew that she was important to him. He already did.

"I love my room. It's so beautiful and thoughtful and wonderful and..."

He put his finger up to her mouth to stem the flow and leaned down slowly to nibble on her lips. She sighed and opened her mouth to the man she loved. He took possession of her mouth like he had possession of her soul.

"I'm not scared anymore. I want to be your wife." She looked deep into his eyes. "Make love to me, Zach."

He pulled her body close and she could feel his hard erection pressing against her. She sighed when he leaned in and nipped her neck.

"That's what I've been doing all along, baby, each and every time."

"Then take me back to bed."

"What about your arm? Maybe we should wait until you're better."

"You're a Marine, Zach. Improvise, adapt and overcome."

The End

www.ingramcontent.com/pod-product-compliance
Lightning Source LLC
Chambersburg PA
CBHW030545130626
46552CB00006B/2439